The Aztec Heresy

PAUL CHRISTOPHER

THE AZTEC HERESY

CANELO

First published in the United States in 2008 by Signet, an imprint of New American Library, a division of Penguin Group (USA) Inc.

This edition published in the United Kingdom in 2019 by

Canelo Digital Publishing Limited
57 Shepherds Lane
Beaconsfield, Bucks HP9 2DU
United Kingdom

A CIP catalogue record for this book is available from the British Library.

Print ISBN 978 1 78863 545 5
Ebook ISBN 978 1 78863 227 0

Look for more great books at www.canelo.co

Printed and bound in Great Britain by Clays Ltd, Elcograf S.p.A.

To Geoff and Deryldene Tucker,
Good Friends from the Rock,
Last of the Old Breed

The Past

1

Sunday, the fifteenth of July, A.D. 1521

Cayo Hueso, Florida

Friar Bartolome de las Casas of the Ordo fratrum Praedicatorum, the Order of St. Dominic, heard the giant wave before he saw it. The surging breaker came out of the storm-wracked darkness like a howling beast, a savage, climbing monster that suddenly appeared behind the treasure-laden galleon *Nuestra Señora de las Angustias*. The wave's belly was as black as the night around it, the huge, driving shoulders a livid sickly green, its ragged, curling head white and torn with ghostly tendrils of wind-whipped spume and spindrift.

It rose like a toppling wall above the stern of the groaning ship, pushing the galleon ahead of it like a chip of wood in a rain-swollen gutter. The seething wave rose until it could rise no more, filling the dark sky above the terrified monk, then reaching down for the ship like some malevolent screaming demon of the seas. Seeing it, Friar

Bartolome knew without a doubt that his life was about to end.

He waited for death helplessly crouched in the waist of the vessel with the other few passengers who had come aboard in Havana, including the boy, Don Antonio Velázquez, the governor's son, who was on his way home to Spain for the education appropriate to a young man of the nobility. Some of the crew were desperately trying to unship the *Nuestra Señora*'s small boats from the skid rails over the main hatch cover while the rest of the men huddled by the fo'c'sle deck. No one stayed below in such desperate weather; better to see fate approaching, no matter how terrible, than to seal yourself blindly within a leaking, unlit coffin.

Above them the rain came down in torrents and the remains of the fore staysail and the foresail hammered in the terrible wind, the lines and rigging beating like hailstones on the drum-heads of torn, ruined canvas. The rest of the sails had been ragged to tatters and the jib-boom was gone entirely and the bowsprit splintered away.

There had to be a hole somewhere deep within the hull because the *Nuestra Señora* was moving more and more sluggishly with every passing moment and taking water in the stern. The sea anchor was gone, forcing them to run before the wind, any remnant of control long since vanished. The mainmast groaned and creaked, the hull moaned, and the seas pounded mercilessly at the schooner's flanks. Everyone knew the ship wouldn't last the hour, let alone survive the night.

Turning his head in time to see the deadly, bludgeoning wave, Friar Bartolome had a single heartbeat to take some measure to save himself and his precious cargo. With barely a conscious thought he dropped to the sodden deck and wrapped his arms tightly around the anchor chain that lay between the capstan and the bitt, holding on for dear life as the breaking monster pummeled him.

The wave struck with a thundering roar, and an even more terrible sound emerged from within the belly of the ship: a deep, grating screech as the keel scraped along a hidden line of reef and then stuck fast, hard aground, wedged between two invisible clutching jaws of coral. The *Nuestra Señora* stopped dead in the water. There was an immense cracking sound and the mainmast toppled, carrying the yards and spars along with it into the raging sea.

The wave, unhindered, swept along the deck of the schooner, swallowing the cowering crew, demolishing the ship's boats and burying Friar Bartolome beneath tons of suffocating water. The wave surged on, the suction pulling at his straining arms and heavy cassock, but he managed to keep his grip long enough for the great green wall to pass. He came up for air and saw in an instant that he was the only one left alive on the deck. Everyone else was gone except the boy, Don Antonio, who now lay broken like a child's doll, tangled in the pins and rigging of the foremast fife rail. His head was crushed, and gray matter oozed wetly from beneath his cap, his eyes wide and staring toward the dark heavens, seeing nothing. There would be no school in Spain after all.

Friar Bartolome looked back toward the stern but saw only the dark. Struggling to his knees, he began tearing at his black cassock, realizing that if he was thrown into the water the drenched fabric would doom him, dragging him down to the bottom. He managed to relieve himself of the heavy robe, and then the next wave struck with no warning at all.

Without the anchor chain to hold him the monk was immediately swept up, turned head over heels and thrown toward the snarled rigging at the bow, striking his head on the rail and feeling a piercing tear at his throat as a splinter of wood slashed into him. Then he was overboard, pushed down so deeply within the wave that he felt the rough touch of the coral bottom as it smashed into his shoulders and back. Crushed by the huge weight of water, he felt the remains of his clothing being torn away and he tumbled helplessly within the wave across the seabed. He forced himself to hold his breath and pushed toward the surface, his arms windmilling underwater, his face upturned.

Finally he broke free of the wave's terrible grip and gulped in huge gasping lungfuls of air, retching seawater, then felt the tug of the next wave as he was swept forward and down again with barely enough time to take a breath before the deluge swallowed him. Once more he was pressed down to the bottom, the rough sand and coral tearing at his skin, and once more, exhausted, he clawed his way to the surface for another retching breath.

A fourth wave took him, but this time instead of coral there was only sand on the sloping bottom, and he barely had to swim at all before he reached the surface. His feet stumbled and he threw himself forward with the last of his strength, staggering as the sea sucked back from the shore in a rushing rip current strong enough to bring him to his knees. He crawled, rose to his feet again and plunged on, knees buckling, in despair because he knew in some distant corner of his mind that another wave as strong as the first could still steal his life away with salvation and survival so tantalizingly near.

He staggered again in the treacherous sand that dragged at his heels and almost toppled over. He took another step and then another, blinking in the slanting, blinding rain. Ahead, farther up the broad strip of shining beach, was a darker line of trees, fan palms and coconuts, their trunks bent away from the howling wind and the lashing rain. Unripe fruit tore away and crashed into the forest like cannonballs. His breath came in ragged gasps and his legs were like deadweights, but at least he was free of the mad, clutching surf that broke behind him now like crashing thunder.

He struggled higher up the sandy slope and finally reached a point above the wrack and turned back to the sea. He sank down exhausted to his knees, naked except for the ragged remnants of his linen stockings and his undershift. He was still badly frightened, but he wept with relief as he stared into the shrieking night. By the grace of God and by the continuing miracles of the most secret and terrible Hounds of God, he had survived.

Through the rain he could see the heaving broken line of frothing white that marked the reef the ship had run aground on, but nothing more. Somewhere out there, invisible in the darkness, the *Nuestra Señora de las Angustias* was dying, breaking apart on the teeth of the coral shore, her crew and captain gone to their fates, leaving Friar Bartolome alone in this terrible place. Remembering suddenly, he fumbled under his remaining clothing and felt for the oilskin-wrapped parcel and its precious contents, which had been strapped securely around his waist. He screamed in frustration against the howling wind. The Codex and the last and greatest secret left by the fiendish heretic and enemy of God, Hernán Cortéz, Marqués del Valle de Oaxaca, was gone.

2

MacDill Air Force Base, Tampa, Florida

Sometimes, like the massive explosion of a hydrogen bomb, two small events, innocuous on their own, can combine to create a terrible result. In this case the two events were a pre-Christmas party at the base, resulting in Major Buck Tynan's pounding hangover, and a corroded turbine pin valve in the port-side outer engine nacelle of the B-47 strategic bomber known as *Mother's Goose.*

It was Tynan's job as aircraft commander and pilot to "box the square," flying the *Goose* in a set pattern from MacDill west to a map coordinate off the Yucatán Peninsula, then southeast to another coordinate off Kingston, Jamaica, a jog east to the Turks and Caicos Island, just barely hitting Cuban airspace at Guantánamo. From the Turks and Caicos he'd then guide *Mother's Goose* back to her nest at MacDill just in time for breakfast. Two eggs, poached, with bacon and home fries.

The whole flight took roughly five hours and at no time was the sleek swept-wing bomber ever more than ninety minutes from its main target in the event of war: Havana. Tynan and a dozen other B-47 crews had been flying the same picket patterns twenty-four hours a day, seven days a week, since the crisis in October, when Kennedy and Khrushchev went nose to nose over the Russian missiles. Between the B-47s at MacDill and the U-2s out of Edwards in California, they had Castro covered.

From the outside *Mother's Goose* was a perfectly stream-lined aerodynamic beauty. From the inside she was as cramped as the inside of a washing machine; certainly no one had thought about the crew when the bird was being designed. The whole cockpit was slightly offset to the right with an eighteen-inch-wide passage along the left. According to people he trusted, the aircraft had been put together over a weekend in a hotel room in Glendale, California, and the original design had been carved out of a chunk of balsa wood from a local hobby shop.

The seating was in tandem, the navigator-bombardier crammed into the nose, the copilot above and behind him, and the pilot behind him, with only the pilot and the copilot under the heavy plastic canopy. In the event of an emergency the navigator ejected downward, which was fine if the aircraft had enough altitude, while the pilot and the copilot ejected upward.

There were no toilet facilities, so the men used makeshift urinals. Coffee in a thermos and wax-paper-wrapped sandwiches were the order of the day as far as food went. The ordnance consisted of two automatically operated cannon in the tail; not much use against Fidel's surface-to-air-missile batteries or anything else you were likely to meet at thirty-nine-thousand feet.

The bomb load was something else again: two twelve-foot, six-inch B-43 MOD-1 thermonuclear devices, each with a one-megaton yield. One of the bombs would turn Havana into a crater. Two would turn the top end of Cuba into a sheet of molten glass. Tynan rarely thought about that sort of thing; his job was to fly the pattern, then go for breakfast. Taking off that night, he was thinking about the party and his splitting headache. The last thing he wanted to do was fly.

For the first hour out of MacDill everything was as usual. Dick Baumann, the navigator, was singing an endless round of "Duke of Earl" while he kept one eye on the compass and the other on his charts. Wally Meng, the copilot, was actually flying the *Goose*, and Tynan was dozing, waiting to take over once they'd made the first leg. Outside was pitch darkness. It was two o'clock in the morning and the joint was definitely not jumping. The only sounds other than Baumann's dubious version of "Duke of Earl" was the monotonous droning roar of the six J-47 engines and the whisper of air passing over the canopy at four hundred and fifty miles an hour. Tynan sighed behind the thick rubber of his mask. He might as well have been on a bus.

The first dark cloud on the horizon was just that—a dark cloud on the horizon. Baumann caught it first on his pint-sized radar screen.

"Major, we got us a storm system dead ahead," said the navigator, his Tennessee drawl crackling in Tynan's headset.

"Did the Met report mention it?"

"No, sir, nuh-huh."

"Idiots."

"That's a roger, Major—it surely is."

"What's it look like?"

"Big. Tropical storm maybe, thirty miles out," said Baumann.

Tynan glanced at the glowing dial of his airspeed indicator: four hundred and twenty miles per hour. Seven miles a minute. Maybe four minutes before they ran right into it. God damn.

"Bit late in the season, isn't it?"

"Sure enough, but that doesn't make it go away, Major."

"Can we get over it?"

"Doubt it. She's a tall one, yes siree."

"Electrical?"

"Most likely," grunted Baumann uneasily. "These Mexican whirligigs usually are." The B-47 was known for its finicky electronics. The last thing Tynan or the others wanted was to ride the *Goose* through a lightning storm with a couple of megaton nucks in the basement.

"Give me a plot that cuts the corner a little, we'll see if we can sneak by."

Yessir," answered Baumann.

Tynan pressed the channel switch on his throat microphone and spoke to Wally Meng, sitting in front of him in the copilot's chair. "I'll take her, Wally," he said. He took the yoke in his left hand. There was a sudden stiffening of the wheel as Meng relinquished control of the big jet.

"You got her," said the copilot.

"Confirmed." Tynan could feel the sweat starting to form under his helmet. Not a bus anymore. A hundred tons of steel and aluminum going half the speed of sound toward a giant light socket in the sky.

"Plot," crackled Baumann from the navigator's compartment in the nose. "Gonna take us ten degrees off course and then we'll have to do a comeback. Cut into our fuel a bit."

"To hell with that. Input the plot."

"Yessir."

Suddenly they were into the outer edges of the storm, rain streaming off the canopy in a sheeting haze that made any kind of visibility impossible. The autopilot had taken the plot and Tynan could feel the oversized pedals moving under his booted feet. The sky lit up as lightning exploded directly in front of them, and Tynan felt a shock of pain lance through his forehead as the sound wave hammered them. The jet shook like a leaf.

At which point the needle valve in the outer port-side nozzle cracked and then disintegrated. The result was instantaneous. The engine exploded, tearing away from its reinforced pylon, releasing a blossoming cloud of high-octane jet fuel and immolating twenty feet of the *Goose*'s left wing.

Loss of power, usually on takeoff, was one of the unsolved problems with the B-47's otherwise excellent stability record. According to the operating handbook for the bomber, a sudden loss of power, especially in the catastrophic way *Mother's Goose* was experiencing, required a 1.7-second response from the pilot to apply full opposite rudder in an effort to prevent the aircraft from cartwheeling, a result of the unequal thrust of the engines on the undamaged wing; 1.7 seconds was well beyond the performance capabilities of Major Buck Tynan's alcohol-soaked mind at the critical moment. By the time he slammed his right foot down on the rudder pedal almost a full three seconds had passed.

He fought for control but it was no use; gravity and physics were having their way with *Mother's Goose*. The end result was inevitable and everyone on the bomber knew it. All three members of the crew reacted instinctively.

In the nose section Baumann grabbed the bicycle brake levers on the right side of his seat and squeezed. The powder charge under the seat blew out the hatch beneath the seat's swivel mechanism and the navigator was sucked out into the darkness.

Unfortunately the harness mechanism on the ejection seat's parachute was torn out of place as the seat was sucked downward. Baumann, screaming all the way down, hurtled thirty seven thousand feet into the dark coastal waters a mile or so off the Yucatán Peninsula without anything to slow his descent. By that time the seat, and Baumann strapped securely into it, had reached terminal velocity. The water's surface had the consistency of granite, and Baumann disintegrated on impact.

Wally Meng didn't fare much better, even though he followed emergency ejection procedures to the letter. He made sure his safety harness was tight, checked to make sure the shoulder harness lock connector was secure, then reached across with his right hand to hit the quick disconnect on the air and communication cables.

Finally he gripped the catapult firing initiator and squeezed. The three powder charges blew in sequence and the chair rocketed upward at eighteen g's of force. His only mistake was his quick reaction. The unlucky copilot assumed that Tynan had already ejected, which was not the case.

The canopy over Wally Meng's head was still intact and in place above him—a curving sheet of high-impact plastic. Meng's helmet smashed into the canopy, cracking both canopy and helmet, the force of impact fracturing Meng's skull like an egg splitting on the side of a cast-iron frying pan. Meng's head, held together now by nothing more than the ruined helmet, was forced up through the canopy and into the four-hundred-mile-an-hour winds that raged across the plastic cowling.

Meng's virtually unprotected neck was bent back by the force of the wind and sawed against the shattered plastic, sending the severed head out into the darkness of the night, spinning away like a gleaming bowling ball and disappearing into the slashing rain.

Tynan eventually came to his senses, getting the jet into some kind of vague control, fighting the pedals and staring at instruments on his panel that were either blinking red or flickering out as the heavy rains swept in through the shattered canopy and shorted everything out.

Things were made even worse by the thick smoke from the ejection-seat charges and the pumping blood spraying up from Wally Meng's headless corpse, still strapped into the smoldering chair. His last glimpse of the altimeter showed that the *Goose* was down to less than two thousand feet and the artificial horizon was showing an amazingly shallow dive.

The engine fire was out but there was no hope for the bomber. The *Goose* was cooked no matter what. At two thousand feet, shallow dive or not, they were going to impact in the next few seconds. He checked his harness, blew the canopy, closed his eyes, and said one extremely dirty word that would definitely have shocked his wife if he'd had one. Then he squeezed the trigger and flew up into the dark, rain-filled sky above the jungles of the Yucatán.

The Present

3

Finn Ryan sat on a hard bench in one of the immense reading rooms of the General Archives of the Indies in Seville, Spain, while her business partner and friend, Lord Billy Pilgrim, went over yet another yellowed piece of parchment with a Sherlock Holmes–sized magnifying glass. Before Finn was an open laptop, two technologies side by side separated by five hundred years.

"You'd think the monks who transcribed these things would have had better penmanship," grumbled Billy, bent low over the manuscript.

"You're the one who took Spanish literature at Oxford," Finn said and smiled.

"Literature, not laundry lists," said Billy. "Which is exactly what these chicken scratchings are. Cargo lists, passenger lists, bills of lading, memos from one bureaucrat to another on the state of the sugar industry. It's bloody boring, it is."

"As Indiana Jones says in *The Last Crusade*, 'Most of archaeology is done in the library.'"

"Bugger Indiana Jones," responded her blond companion. "You didn't see him sitting about peering at old bits of parchment in dusty rooms in a mausoleum of a place like this. He ran about cracking his whip, fighting off rats and snakes and shooting people. Much more fun, if you ask me."

"Give me the dusty rooms any day," answered Finn. "I've had enough of the other to last me for a while."

"I suppose you're right," agreed Billy. Their last adventure had seen them attacked in the Underground in London, his boat blown out of the water in an Amsterdam marina, their lives almost forfeit in a China Sea typhoon, and being cast away on a desert island off the northern coast of Borneo with the descendants of a crew of ancient Chinese warriors. And that was just the beginning of their troubles.

"Getting back to what we're here for, what do the old memos and bills of lading say about the *Nuestra Señora de las Angustias*?" Finn asked.

"That she was caught in a hurricane in the middle of July in 1521 and sank like a stone in the waters just off Key West, which they called Cayo Hueso back then—Island of Bones. Six months later a salvage ship, the *Nuestra Señora de la Concepción*, otherwise known as *Cagafuego* by her crew, was sent from Havana to salvage the treasure, which was considerable."

"*Cagafuego*?" Finn said.

"Roughly translated it means 'Fireshitter,' if you must know."

"Forget I asked," replied Finn. "What happened then?"

"They salvaged just about everything, which is why the wreck has been ignored; there's nothing on it. They also managed to pick up a survivor from the original ship, the *Nuestra Señora de las Angustias*. A fellow named Friar Bartolome de las Casas, a Dominican. The name pops up a number of times. He must have been quite important."

"I wonder if it's a coincidence," Finn said.

"Coincidence?"

"My father used to talk about someone with the same name all the time when he was on his digs in Mexico and Central America when I was a kid," she explained. "*That* Bartolome de las Casas was a Dominican as well. He was one of the friars who invaded Mexico with Cortéz; in fact, he was confessor to Cortéz, knew all his secrets, including the location of the hidden temple in the Yucatán where Montezuma hid the bulk of his treasure. Cortéz was afraid that the royal court back in Spain was setting him up as a heretic with the Inquisition just to steal the gold and jewels, so he never told anyone where this mythical city was. Everyone in the Mexican colony searched for it for more than a hundred years and then it was forgotten, turned into myth, cursed, in fact." Finn shrugged. "There was supposed to be some Codex involved but that's turned into a myth as well."

23

"Codex?"

"They were books, sort of, long accordion-folded strips full of Aztec pictograms painted on *amatl* paper—pounded fig bark. One of the most famous is the Florentine Codex. The Spanish Inquisition tried to have it destroyed and almost succeeded. Another one is the Boturini Codex, which was written by an unknown Aztec only a decade or so after the conquest by Cortéz. There are about a dozen of them all told. They're spread all over the place now. Princeton, the National Library in Paris, a library in Florence."

"How about the Vatican?" Billy asked, staring through the magnifying glass at the faded parchment in front of him.

"One of the most famous, the Codex Borgia. Why?"

"This manuscript keeps on mentioning something called the *Cavallo Nero* and the Vatican, along with the phrase *'Tira de la Ciudad Dorado de Cortéz'*—Strip Concerning Cortéz's City of Gold. Could that be one of these Codex things you seem to know so much about?"

"It sounds like it. *Cavallo Nero* is Italian. It means Black Knight, as in the chess piece," Finn said and nodded, excitement rising in her voice.

"Some sort of secret society?"

"I wouldn't be surprised," said Finn. "Especially if it involves the Dominicans. They were the driving force behind the Inquisition. Always snooping around. Sort of a religious Gestapo. Fifteenth-century Homeland Security."

"But that's Spain, not Rome," Billy said.

Finn shook her head. "Everyone thinks the Inquisition originated in Spain. It didn't. It started in the Vatican. Pope Sixtus the Fourth, the man who built the Sistine Chapel and re-founded the Vatican Library. The Inquisition still exists, except now it's called the Congregation for the Doctrine of the Faith. It's the oldest department in the Vatican."

"The Black Knights. Sounds ominous," said Billy.

"If they were Dominicans and they were involved in the Inquisition, they probably weren't the good guys, that's for sure," agreed Finn. She drummed her fingers on the table in front of her. "I wonder if it's still there," she murmured.

"What's still where?"

"The *Tira de la Ciudad Dorado de Cortéz*," said Finn. "I wonder if it's still in the Vatican Library."

"Maybe it never got there," answered Billy almost hopefully.

"The City of Gold," said Finn, her voice slow. "My father always believed it existed. It was his Holy Grail."

"I thought Sir Galahad found the Holy Grail, then Monty Python, and then Dan Brown."

"You forgot Indiana Jones," said Finn absently.

"You've got quite a thing for him," said Billy. "Or is it Harrison Ford?"

"Ssshh," whispered Finn. "I'm thinking."

Billy Pilgrim shifted uneasily on the hard wooden bench. "Why is it I get this terrible feeling of impending doom?" he asked.

"Don't be such an old fuddy-duddy." Finn laughed. "Let's go find the Seville version of a Starbucks and talk about this City of Gold."

Twenty minutes later a young man in an open-neck white shirt and jeans strolled into the Plaza de la Alianza. He was carrying a small video camera in his hand. He looked like a tourist, which, in a sense, was exactly what he was.

The plaza was small and intimate, one side taken up completely with the crumbling brick and stone rear of the church that sat on the street parallel to the plaza. The other three sides of the patterned stone square were taken up with small businesses, including a Starbucks on one corner. Small orange trees had been planted for shade around the square and were all bearing bright orange fruit.

In the center of the square was a small simple fountain of the kind you could see in a thousand squares like the plaza, which could be found throughout the city. There were tables and chairs lined up against the wall of the old church, and the young man sat down and began to swing his camera in a slow pan around the square.

He seemed to pay particular attention to the Starbucks, which occupied the main floor of a two-storied white-washed building. He zoomed in and held on a couple seated at one of the café tables in front of the coffee shop. He carefully zoomed closer, then held the shot until he was sure he had enough footage of the couple. They were talking together quite earnestly. The man was blond with the body of a swimmer, broad-shouldered and narrow-hipped. The woman was slim with long red hair, as beautiful as a Pre-Raphaelite painting of *The Lady of Shalott*.

The young man in the white shirt panned around the plaza a second time, just for effect, and then put the camera down on the little table in front of him. He took a cell phone out of the pocket of his shirt, he dialed the international telephone code, the Italian country code, and finally the 379 area code. He entered a seven-digit number. It was answered on the third ring.

"Yes?" The language was Italian, the tone careful and considered. A voice with power behind it.

"I have them," the young man in the plaza answered. "Our contact in the Archives of the Indies said they have been looking for references that include information about the Codex."

"Interesting," said the man on the other end of the call. "That makes two interested parties in the past month."

"What shall I do?" asked the man in the white shirt.

27

"Nothing. Keep them under surveillance for the time being."

"Yes, Your Eminence."

"The opening moves have begun," said the voice. "We are in play again after a very long time. We must be patient now."

"Yes, Your Eminence."

"If they become too curious, remove them from the board. Keep me advised."

Remove them from the board, thought the young man. *In other words, kill them.*

The cell phone went dead in the young man's ear. He put the phone back in his shirt pocket and watched the couple outside the Starbucks. He inhaled the sweet fragrance of the orange trees and began to pray for the souls of the couple at the table beyond the fountain.

4

Max Kessler lived at 3307 N Street NW in Georgetown, Washington, D.C., two doors down from the corner of Thirty-third Street and two blocks north of the shops and restaurants of M Street. The house was one of those rare addresses in Georgetown: a single-family dwelling on its own plot of ground. For Max Kessler this was the best feature of the residence; the thought of sharing a wall with another building almost made him nauseous.

Its other great attraction was the fact that it had been occupied by Jack Kennedy from 1958 until his ascension to the White House. Sometimes late at night, when Max did some of his best sorting and shifting, he was sure that he could hear the faint voices of Jack and Jackie in conversation or smell Jackie's Creed's Fleurissimo perfume, the scent created for Grace Kelly. Sometimes he was equally sure he could smell the rich smoke from the short-lived president's cigars. In every other way a practical and phlegmatic man, Maxmillian Alois Kessler fully believed that his house was haunted by the spirits of these two great Americans.

Max Kessler was born in the Gasthaus Monika in the southern Bavarian mining town of Miesbach, Germany. The date of his birth was April 30, 1945, the same day Adolf Hitler put a gun to his head and committed suicide in Berlin. Max's father called himself Kurt Von Kessler, although he had no right to use the term of nobility.

Kurt Von Kessler, noble or not, was a colonel in the SS and senior assistant to Reinhard Gehlen, the Nazi staff officer and intelligence chief who had been in charge of all espionage activities within the Soviet Union during the course of World War II.

As the war wound down in Germany, Gehlen the spymaster and his organization moved into the Bavarian Alps to wait for the Americans to arrive, which accounted for Max's rural birth. When Gehlen and his group were hired on by the fledgling CIA, Kurt Kessler, minus the "Von," was brought to America along with his wife and child under the notorious Operation Paperclip, which saw hundreds of Nazis brought to America during the immediate postwar years, some of them who could only be described as war criminals.

Kurt Kessler, along with his old boss Gehlen, settled in Washington, D.C., and became a specialist in South American and Central American intelligence gathering, since he had many contacts with scores of old friends who were now living there.

Kurt's son, Max, was raised as an American, went to American schools, and graduated from Georgetown University with high honors, specializing in South American affairs and languages. He then took a postgraduate degree in Soviet political science. He spoke English, Spanish, Portuguese, Russian, and Czech with equal and perfect fluency. Of course, he also spoke the High German of his father like a native Berliner.

His mother and father were killed in an automobile accident in 1968 just after he obtained his postgraduate degree. Within two weeks of burying his parents, Max was recruited by the Central Intelligence Agency.

He turned down the offer, preferring to maintain both his autonomy and his privacy, and set himself up as a consultant working as a broker between American and South American business interests and as a private advisor on Soviet affairs, specializing in trade agreements with Eastern Bloc countries.

Using his parents' insurance money and his own trust fund, Max Kessler purchased the house in Georgetown and had lived there ever since, maintaining it as both home and office. He never married, had no hobbies, pastimes, or friends. He never met with clients or anyone else at the house on N Street and never cooked there, preferring to eat all his meals at any one of an endless supply of restaurants on M Street. Work was everything, knowledge was everything, information was everything. Power was everything.

Max had inherited more than money and a facility with languages from his father. He had also inherited his father's obsessive need to catalogue and order every facet of his life. His last inheritance was less ephemeral than the others: he had inherited his father's files, *Der Wunderkasten*, as Kurt Kessler called them, the Magic Boxes.

The boxes, five hundred of them, each held a thousand three-by-five index cards, each card having a neatly typed entry of up to one hundred and fifty coded words summarizing one of Reinhard Gehlen's private files on agents and activities from Vladivostok to Moscow and from Leningrad to Odessa.

Originally intended to be nothing more than a backup to the originals in case of accident or fire, the cards eventually became a ticket out of the horrors that came with the end of the war. Gehlen's own file copies of his records filled three large trucks when the Gehlen Organization fled to Miesbach; Kurt Kessler, seeing the collapse of Hitler's Germany even before Gehlen, had called in a favor or two with the Luftwaffe reconnaissance people and had his index cards photographed under an animation camera at what was left of one of the UFA film labs in Berlin. His half million index cards were spirited out of Germany in three large film cans that could easily be carried in a single suitcase.

Using his father's filmed files as the basis for his own system, and the extensive fallout shelter Jack Kennedy had secretly built in the basement of the house on N Street, Max Kessler added to his patrimony with coded files of his own. In the first ten years he doubled the size of his father's files, and over the next ten years he quadrupled the number.

Even with the advent of computers, nothing changed in the private world of Max Kessler. Each card was typed on a sturdy IBM Executive and the tape ribbons were individually destroyed in the living room fireplace as they were used. In 1990 he purchased a Kodak rotary microfilm camera and installed it in the basement, slowly but surely transferring his file cards to film, just like his father had.

From that point on he kept only the last five years' worth of cards on hand, archiving the rest. Nowhere in the house was there a copy of the code Max Kessler used to input his information onto the cards. The individual file drawers stacked in the basement were all locked and alarmed, as was the microfilm storage area of archived cards, which occupied a fireproof vault that was also connected to Max Kessler's alarm system. The bomb shelter entrance was itself disguised as well as being locked and alarmed.

As a further element of his efficient system he micro-filmed each and every check given to him by his clients, invariably depositing the checks into a rotating and ever-changing series of banks in several states, then transferring the funds to a bank in Switzerland that he still considered to be the most discreet, despite their recent problems regarding Holocaust accounts. Max and his father had shared the same account at Baer & Cie, Geneva, since 1945, the year of Max Kessler's birth, without any problems or indiscretions. His father had dealt directly with Joseph Baer and Max dealt with his son, Fritz.

To Max Kessler trust was anathema. There was only a single attic window on the east and west sides of the house, and both the front and rear windows were covered in polarizing film. The laneway at the back was a dead end and the cameras at the rear of the house were all infrared. He swept his house every day for electronic bugs, had a total of six other digital surveillance cameras installed on the outside of his house, and had never even considered using a cell phone or a PDA. One of his professors at Georgetown University had once commented on the neat, tiny handwriting of his essays to a fellow professor as being the work of an antisocial anal-retentive Luddite. Most of his fellow students simply thought of him as a freak and kept out of his way.

On this particular day Max Kessler was having lunch at Leopold's, a small café-restaurant in the courtyard off Cady's Alley, a narrow pedestrian walkway just off M Street. He was having his regular afternoon meal: *Miesmuscheln*—mussels in white wine and herbed potatoes—

to be followed by *Mohr im Hemdt*—chocolate mousse with hazelnut ice cream—and finishing with a German coffee, coffee with Kirschwasser cherry brandy, sugar, and whipped cream, the only time he drank anything alcoholic.

At five minutes to two Max Kessler finished his meal and paid for it, leaving an appropriate tip, then walked back down Cady's Alley to M Street. At exactly 2:00 p.m. a black Lincoln Town Car slid down M Street, driving west, and pulled over to the curb directly in front of Kessler. He opened the rear door, entered the car, and sat back against the black leather seat.

"Site Three," said Max, and the car moved off. Site Three was a park bench on the Mall directly in front of the National Museum of Natural History and directly across from the red-brick Smithsonian Castle, and getting there involved some complicated maneuvering up and down Washington's maze of one-way streets. The car dropped him off in front of the museum on the Madison Drive side, and Kessler walked across the street and turned onto the broad gravel path. As usual the grass on the Mall was spotty, brown with neglect and burnt by too much sun, dog urine, and excrement, not to mention the litter, which wasn't surprising in a post-9/11 world, where trash containers were a potential target for hordes of brown-skinned terrorists and had all been removed years ago.

He glanced up the Mall toward the Capitol. That, of course, was where the real terrorists could be found, in Congress and the Senate. The terrorism of Greed and Stupidity, Kessler called it. He smiled. No matter; he had files on each and every one of them and had made a great deal of money from them as clients, trading secrets of the one to the curiosity of the other.

Kessler sat down on the designated bench, folded his small hands in his lap, and waited. Five minutes later his client-to-be sat down beside him. He was a large man, tall, broad-shouldered, and well dressed in a tailored suit that made him look like a lawyer or a banker. His skin was very tanned, his brownish hair streaked by a lot of sun, his eyes light blue and hard.

"What do you know about Angel Guzman?" asked the hard-eyed man.

"A great deal," said Kessler, who'd done his research.

"Tell me."

"He's a Mexican warlord. On his father's side he is the illegitimate grandson of Dr. Arnulfo Arias, the three-time president of Panama. On his mother's side he is the grandson of a *puta*, a whore from Mexico City. He is considered to be completely insane. He collects the mutilated sex organs of his enemies the way soldiers in Vietnam collected ears. He is the last of the great *cocainistas*, men like Pablo Escobar. He wants to use all his money and power to make the Yucatán a separate state, and after that he thinks he can spawn a new Mexican Revolution. The general consensus is that he wants to be king." Max Kessler stopped.

"Is that it?" said the man beside him. "I could have got that much off Wikipedia."

"That is most certainly not all," answered Kessler. "The file on Señor Guzman is a considerable one and very detailed. Sex habits, his curious concern for his bowels. His fear of escalators. His private radio codes. The names of the key people in his organization both in Mexico and in other places, the location of his headquarters in the jungles of Quintana Roo."

"Jesus, you know all that?"

"And more." Kessler nodded.

"How do I get my hands on the information?"

"By paying me a great deal of money."

"How much?"

"Two hundred and fifty thousand dollars," said Kessler blandly.

"A little steep, isn't it?"

"You can afford it."

"That's irrelevant. It's still a lot of money."

"Then don't pay it."

"Your father was a Nazi, right?"

"Three hundred thousand dollars," murmured Kessler.

"All right. When can I get the file?"

"As soon as you give me the money," said Kessler.

"Half when I get the file, half when I've read it."

"Don't be silly," said Kessler. "All of it when I put the file in your hands. Hard copy, microfiche, or microfilm. Scanned onto a memory stick, if you prefer, it's all the same to me." The scanner was Kessler's only nod to twenty-first-century technology, but it had become necessary simply for the sake of transportability.

"You've got to be joking!" the man exclaimed. "You expect me to pay you that kind of money, sight unseen?"

"I expect nothing," said Kessler, standing. "And I never joke. Ask your father. Three hundred and fifty thousand dollars."

"You said three hundred!"

"I don't like your tone," said Kessler. "Let me know what you decide." He glanced at his watch. The car would be waiting outside the museum in a minute or two. He turned away from the bench and headed back down the path. A Rottweiler on a leash was squatting on the grass, having a gargantuan bowel movement; the creature's owner, a pretty young woman in a flowered skirt and sweater, was looking on like a proud parent, a clear plastic bag wrapped inside-out around her hand. Kessler wondered if she'd noticed there wasn't a trash bin for miles around.

He reached the loading zone in front of the museum just as the Lincoln reappeared. He climbed into the rear of the car and gave the driver his instruction.

"Home, please."

The driver nodded and pulled smoothly away from the curb. Kessler sank back against the leather once again. He closed his eyes. A good lunch and an interesting meeting. It demonstrated one of his father's favorite credos when it came to intelligence gathering: sometimes the questions asked were more useful than the answers. Why did Harrison Noble, the dilettante owner of Noble Ventures, a treasure-hunting company, and the son of the pharmaceutical billionaire James Jonas Noble, want detailed information on a Mexican thug and drug lord based in the wilds of the Yucatán jungle? And why now?

5

Capitán de Navío Arkady Tomas Cruz stood at the wheel of the stinking old fish boat and smoked a cigarette. Behind him the few lights of the village he used as a navigation marker were beginning to fade on the far side of the bay. He adjusted his course a little, feeling the helm sluggishly answer to the motion of the wheel.

The boat was the Cuban version of a classic North Carolina Core Sounder with a low, graceful sheer sweeping up to a flared bow, while the after end was almost daintily curved, offering no sharp edges to snag the nets. There was a simple cabin forward that sheltered a minimal galley, a pair of berths, and a bad-weather steering station with a hatchlike windowed box for the helmsman to look around. The boat was thirty-five feet long and carried a rusted old Guantánamo province registration plate on the bow. The name *Panda* was roughly painted in black on the stern. It was most definitely not Arkady Tomas Cruz's usual command.

Arkady Tomas was a hybrid with the dark, tanned, almost Indio looks of his Cuban father and the high cheekbones and bright blue eyes of his Russian mother. His parents had met in Russia, his father a student at the First Leningrad Medical Institute, his mother a physicist at the Admiralty Shipyards, which dated back to the times of the czars. Arkady spent his early years in Leningrad, journeying back to Cuba once a year with his father but never quite feeling as though he belonged.

He spoke Spanish well, but not quite like a native, and somehow the coldness of the country of his birth seemed to infuse itself into his personality, making him shy and distant. He graduated from the Nachimovsky Naval School in 1984 and in 1986 from the Higher Naval School for Submariners. He spent the early part of his career on both Juliet and Foxtrot submarines, and on the death of his mother in 1992 he returned to Cuba with his father. From 1993 until their decommissioning he was in overall command of the four Foxtrot submarines in the Cuban fleet.

By 2000 that fleet was down to one active submarine doing occasional coastal patrols, and by 2004 the last sub was rated as inactive, although there were some rumors that it had sunk somewhere in the Windward Passage and had been lost with all hands. For Arkady during that time there had been a brief marriage of no account to a woman named Marina Gelfriel, who worked as a junior curator at the Hermitage, but since most of his time was spent in the northern bases like Vidyaevo, a hundred miles north of Murmansk beyond the Arctic Circle, the marriage was doomed to icy failure from the start. Thankfully there had been no children.

Arkady Tomas looked toward the headland a mile or so away. Dense jungle, and even this far out in the water he could taste the stink of it in his nostrils, like hot steam pouring off some cooking broth. He smiled, feeling the sweat in his armpits and along his spine, still able to remember the white, frozen hell of the Kola Peninsula; the place he'd once thought of as his home. He ducked his head and lit another Popular. He held the cigarette between his teeth against the wind and turned the wheel another couple of points to round the headland and guide the boat into the next bay.

Ahead of him now, half a mile away, was the rusting hulk of a ship, a sour jarring geometry against the wall of convoluted, color-splashed jungle that served as its backdrop. The wreck stood two hundred yards or so off the ragged empty shore, stern in, torn in half when she foundered. The bow section was ripped away, sunk into the deeper waters beyond the shoals where the wreck now lay.

Arkady Tomas Cruz knew the ship's history well. She was the SS *Atlantic Champion*, also known as the SS *Angela Harrison* in her later years, built by the Welding Shipyards in Kure, Japan, in 1954 for National Bulk Carriers and the largest tanker afloat at the time of her construction.

She was originally 854 feet long and 125 feet wide, with a spindly four-story-high navigation bridge in the forward section and a lower deckhouse aft. Luckily, at the time of her demise in 1974, she had been under tow to the scrap yards in Spain and had spilled no cargo on the Golfo de Guacanayabo shore. Her owners, by then a Panamanian company, had made no attempt to salvage her, given the difficulties of dealing with the Cuban government. After having anything of value stripped from her by local entrepreneurs, she languished for a decade, slowly settling, becoming part of the landscape, invisible except to fresh eyes.

The *Panda* grumbled slowly into the looming shadow of the massive tanker and Arkady Tomas breathed in the scent of iron and peeling paint that had baked in the hot, unrelieved sunlight throughout the daylight hours. He grinned; the interior of the hull would have been a furnace for most of the day, only now cooling to a reasonable temperature. The privileges of rank.

He turned the wheel a few degrees, disappearing around the flank of the tanker on the windward side. The huge wall of rotting steel now stood between him and possible watching eyes on the shore. Twenty yards along he saw the gaping hole in the ship's side, turned the wheel slightly once more, and guided the *Panda* inside the yawning cavern of the old ship's hull.

With almost idiotic irony the idea had come from a James Bond movie. Produced in 1977, three years after the grounding of the SS *Angela Harrison* off the beaches of Baracoa, the film's plot revolved around a giant supertanker that swallowed submarines. The idea that a supertanker could open up its bow section and inhale a couple of nuclear subs was obviously science fiction. The idea that a wrecked tanker on an isolated coast could camouflage an active base for a Russian-Cuban Foxtrot-class submarine was not. In the mid '80s, while there was still money in the Soviet coffers, the hull of the old tanker had been gutted and refitted as a staging base for covert submarine patrols. By the time of the fall of the Soviet Union and the beginning of what Castro began calling the Difficult Times, there was barely any reason for a Cuban navy, let alone four expensive-to-operate examples of what was already an outmoded class of nonnuclear submarine; there was, however, a reason to keep one of them: Admiralty Shipyard's Hull B-510, launched on October 20, 1983, and handed over to the Cuban Revolutionary Navy in February of the following year. The reason was as ironic and fundamentally ludicrous as the plot for the James Bond Movie *The Spy Who Loved Me.*

Since 1972 the United States Navy, in conjunction with the CIA and the American Telephone and Telegraph Company, had been tapping the Soviet telephone cables in the Sea of Okhotsk and the Barents Sea using induction recording equipment that was serviced as regularly as a mailman's route. For a decade the Americans had been listening in on secret military communications between Soviet naval bases and their superiors in Moscow. Eventually, late in 1982, the Soviets discovered the so-called tap-pods, which had numerous parts within them stamped "Made in the U.S.A." Even though the taps had been discovered, it was still regarded as one of the great intelligence coups of the Cold War. The Americans, in their inevitable arrogance, had never considered that the same thing might be done to them.

The arrogance wasn't entirely misplaced. Most secure military and intelligence communications outside the United States were carried on encrypted satellite signals, and had been since Telstar and the earliest telecommunications satellites of the sixties. There was only one place where this was not the case: Havana.

The U.S. Special Interest Section of the Swiss embassy knew perfectly well that the huge Signals Intelligence Center at Lourdes, just beyond the airport, was capable of trapping and tracing any satellite calls made to the mainland, so the nine heavily encrypted high-speed data lines running out of the embassy used the original Cuban American Telephone and Telegraph cable that ran from Havana Harbor to Key West, coming to the surface in a concrete conduit between Fort Zachary Taylor Park and Whitehead Spit. The cable, installed in 1921, was still the only direct-dial link between the two countries. Turnabout was fair play and Cuban intelligence had been tapping the cable since 1986, using the Foxtrot B-510 to service the intercept.

Once every ninety days the submarine would leave the safety of its iron nest, follow the Old Bahamas Channel northwest to the Florida Straits, and take up a position at the thirty-fathom line between Old Man Key and Key West. It was the previous mission to the tap that had provided the initial red flag for a DEA-Coast Guard sweep, and that in turn had led to Arkady's unscheduled visit to the SS *Angela Harrison*.

Cruz eased back even more on the *Panda*'s throttle as he slipped in through the gaping hole in the old ship's side. His eyes adjusted quickly to the sudden dimming of the light as he passed into the cavernous hold. The B-510, all 299 feet of her, was snugged up against the concrete berth that had been constructed to accommodate her on the leeward side of the *Angela Harrison*'s hull. Like most of the old Russian cold-water submarines, she'd been originally painted a dull gray-black. Operating in Caribbean waters, she had wisely been painted over with a high-quality nonreflective and much lighter blue. Surfaced, even in broad daylight, the B-510 was almost invisible from anything more than five hundred yards.

Cruz gazed fondly up at his sinister-looking command, her squat conning tower studded with periscopes and snorkel equipment, her bows, now at low tide, revealing the torpedo tubes carved the same way as an old Buick Roadmaster, like the taxi his cousin Pascual drove in Havana. Unlike most of the modern nuclear-powered missile submarines, the B-510 retained the narrow, fleet look of her immediate ancestor, the German Type XXI of the Kriegsmarine developed at the end of World War II. The B-510's hull configuration, basic design, and even her diesel and electric engines were much the same as the old Nazi boat's, probably because they'd been conceived by the same engineers. The biggest difference was the lack of deck armament. The Type XXI had carried two antiaircraft guns, fore and aft; the B-510 had no weaponry at all beyond a few personal small arms on board and the six forward torpedo tubes and the two tubes aft: *Pedo y Pinga*, as the crew called them—the fart and the dick. Not that it mattered much; there wasn't much an antiaircraft gun could do against an F-18. Unlike most submarines and other vessels in what had once been the Soviet navy and the remnants of the Cuban navy, the B-510 had been given a name, *Babaloo*, written in bold black letters on her bow. On the conning tower there was a cartoon of Desi Arnaz playing the congas and, in English, the words "Honey, I'm Home!" The name and the cartoon, surprisingly enough, had been laughingly confirmed by the Great One himself.

Arkady switched off the *Panda*'s engine and let the small boat slide through the inky, oily water until it bumped against the old truck tires arranged as fenders along the concrete dock. His first officer, Enrico Ramirez, was supervising the loading of the *Babaloo*'s cargo: a dozen 65-76 "Whale" torpedoes, each one packed with 921 pounds of high-grade heroin where there normally would have been an explosive charge. The heroin was manufactured from the highest-grade Afghani opium, which was shipped to a government pharmaceutical lab in Zengcheng, China, where it was processed first into morphine and then into heroin. From there it was sent to the Pearl River port of Xintang, where it was loaded onto any one of a number of China Ocean Shipping Company vessels scheduled for off-loading in Cuba, generally bulk carriers of grain or smaller break-bulk carriers of mixed cargo. Arriving in the port of Manzanillo on the south coast of Cuba, the heroin was then packed into the old Soviet torpedoes for loading onto *Babaloo*. The grain and the heroin were paid in barter for sugar, and the heroin was then transshipped to the Yucatán aboard the Foxtrot for final delivery across the border into the United States. With the early-warning system provided by the regular phone taps in Key West, the system was foolproof. No Coast Guard ship would dare to stop a Chinese government vessel on the high seas, and since the Cuban navy no longer had any submarines, nobody was looking for one. Like any criminal activity of that size, there had been leaks every now and again, but the conspiracy was so involved and far-fetched that even the wildly paranoid Drug Enforcement Agency dismissed the rumors as addle-brained myths. If six-thousand-pound shipments of heroin really were regularly chugging their way underwater across the Caribbean like so much dirty laundry, they might as well hang up their badges and go home. Even if it was happening they didn't want to think about it. Neither did Arkady Cruz. He'd never seen himself as a drug dealer, and his involvement with a madman like the megalomaniac Angel Guzman was repulsive. On the other hand, it was Guzman's hard cash that kept the old Foxtrot seaworthy, and Arkady Tomas Cruz was willing to play Faust to Guzman's Lucifer if it meant keeping the *Babaloo* afloat.

He tied off the *Panda* and went up the stained concrete steps to the pier. He paused to light yet another Popular, then crossed to the winch, where Ramirez was watching as the big gray torpedoes were being loaded through the forward hatch.

"How goes it, Rico?"

"Well enough. Not much warning. These weren't supposed to go out for another two weeks."

"Don't complain. We get to go for an unexpected cruise."

"*Muy bueno*, I get to listen for AWACS and Coast Guard sonar pings for thirty-six hours in a boat full of the stink of fifty men sharing two showers and three toilets." He paused, thinking for a moment, then shook his head. "Make that two toilets. The forward one isn't flushing again."

Arkady Tomas laughed. "Put Payo on toilet paper rations. The *sargento* is the one who plugs it all the time." The truth of course was that the *Babaloo* was old, getting close to thirty, and was never intended to cruise the tropics. She was a cold-water boat and she was aging quickly. "When can we get under way?" he asked, pinching out the Popular and flicking the butt into the black oily water lapping against the concrete pier.

"Call it three hours," said Ramirez. "Just after dark. The tide will be at its highest and it will be dark enough."

"There is no darkness anymore," grumbled Arkady. "They fly those Predator drones like mosquitoes with infrared eyes. I want you to dive the boat as soon as we're over the reef."

"Aye aye, *Amiral*," said Ramirez.

"*Amiral*, my ass," said Arkady Tomas, grinning back at his old friend.

6

"Tell me again why we're driving down the M1-11 in the fog on a visit to a theological college in Cambridge," said Billy, squinting through the windshield of the Renault Laguna they'd rented at Heathrow. "Something about a Jewish Franciscan monk from Switzerland who was friends with a typewriter salesman during World War Two, wasn't it?"

"He wasn't a typewriter salesman. His name was Olivetti. He *made* typewriters. Millions of them."

"But the Franciscan monk was Jewish, right? And a spy as well?"

"You're teasing me," said Finn.

"I'm in awe of you," said Billy Pilgrim. "To the undiscerning eye you appear to be an attractive woman in her late twenties with a pleasant disposition and a lovely smile, when in fact you are a time bomb, ticking away toward your next explosion. Your life appears to be an endless game of hares and hounds and one is never quite sure which is the hare and which is the hound."

"But I'm not boring—you have to admit that," she said and smiled at her friend.

"Boring? No. Quite exciting, actually. One minute we're being shot at in the middle of London and the next minute we're battling Malay pirates side by side with a modern-day Robinson Crusoe obsessed with cheese."

"You're making it sound crazy on purpose," said Finn. "It wasn't that strange."

"No, no," said Billy airily, "just another day at the office for our girl Fiona." He squinted. "What does that sign say?"

"A-1134," answered Finn.

"Bloody hell," said Billy, throwing the wheel to the right. The big Renault rose to the occasion and they lurched onto the exit ramp.

They made their way through the foggy, rather narrow streets of Cambridge, students in little groups appearing through the mist like ghostly flitting bats in their academic gowns. The occasional car went by, its headlights like the glowing yellow eyes of an owl surprised in flight. "The whole place seems deserted," commented Finn. "No people, no traffic. It's like a ghost town."

"Mid-June," explained Billy. "End of term. Everyone's going home for the hols except for the swots."

"Swots?"

"Nose-to-the-grindstone suck-ups, brownnosers who've offered to do scut work for their professors."

"Just like Columbus, Ohio," said Finn with a smile.

"Tush and pish, Miss Ryan. I bet you were a swot yourself."

"Never. If I wasn't off on a dig with my parents I was working at Mickey-D's, just like the rest of my friends, and getting tanked on Saturday night."

"Fiona Ryan as a bad girl," said Billy. "Hard to imagine." He squinted through the windscreen. "Bloody hell," he muttered again.

"It's on a street called Ridley Hall Road," said Finn, looking down at the map of Cambridge in the Blue Guide. They reached the end of the Fen Causeway, then turned right. "Off Malting Lane."

"That's not far from the old Granta Pub," said Billy. "Good shepherd's pie if I remember my school days."

"I thought you went to Oxford."

"But I had a lady friend in Cambridge."

"What happened to her?"

"Sadly she couldn't abide boats. She married a doctor and moved to New Zealand. Rather a rich gynecologist's wife than an impoverished duchess, I suppose."

"Turn here," said Finn, pointing to the left. A street appeared, wisps of fog caught in the branches of a row of ancient alder trees. "Right this time," she said a few seconds later. And then they were on Ridley Hall Road.

"Hardly rates as a road," said Billy, pulling the car to a stop. "Only a block long." On their left was a big slate-roofed institutional building, added to over the decades in varying shades and styles of brickwork that went from dark red to pale yellow, windows from Victorian arched through midcentury sash and modern thermopane.

"That has to be Ridley Hall," said Finn.

"Which makes *that* the residence of our mysterious Franciscan," said Billy, nodding to his right. "Poplar Cottage."

"I don't see any poplars," said Finn, ducking down to look through Billy's window. "And I wouldn't call that a cottage." The house opposite Ridley Hall was a large, slightly sooty-looking place with half a dozen eaves and at least that many chimney pots sprouting up from every corner. It was two and a half stories, covered in a nicotine-colored stucco, the windows tall, arched, and covered with what appeared to be heavy drapes. It was the sort of place where the upstanding citizenry in Sherlock Holmes stories lived, or a suspicious-looking clergyman in an Agatha Christie tale. As though to offset the building's slightly dowdy outward appearance, the narrow front garden was a riot of color, flowers blooming everywhere.

Finn and Billy climbed out of the car and went up the flagstone path. The arched, planked oak doorway had huge wrought-iron hinges and a lion's-head knocker. Below the knocker was a worn-looking brass plate that read: Br. Luca Pacioli.

"Doesn't sound very Jewish to me," said Billy.

After a moment the door swung open and an old man in a cardigan and twill trousers peered out at them over the lenses of a pair of bright red reading glasses. The man had long, snow white hair and a Vandyke beard, neatly trimmed. He looked like Santa Claus on a diet for the summer. He appeared to be in his eighties, but fit enough. In one hand he held an old briar pipe.

"Martin Kerzner?" Finn asked.

The man's eyes widened. "I haven't been called that since the war," he said. "How extraordinary!"

"Matthew Penner from Lausanne sends his regards," said Finn. "My name is Finn Ryan and this is my associate, Billy Pilgrim."

"Brother Matthew. Dear me, I thought he was long dead."

"He said you might be able to answer some questions we had about Friar Bartolome de las Casas and the Order of the Black Knights."

"Well," said the old man, "I know Friar Bartolome is long in his grave, spinning merrily I have no doubt, but the knights are something else altogether." He stepped aside. "Do come in. I'll fix us some tea and biscuits and tell you all about it, if you like."

The interior of the cottage had the same Agatha Christie feel as the exterior. The hallway was dark, paneled wainscoting rising waist-high, the wall above done in a small flower print that had faded to almost nothing. There was a bay-windowed dining room immediately to the left, a kitchen and scullery to the right, and then a dark set of winding stairs leading to the second floor. Beyond the stairs were two more rooms, a drawing room to the left and a library to the right. More wainscoting and wallpaper.

Both the drawing room and the library had small fires burning in the grate and both rooms looked out onto a long narrow garden laid out with half a dozen flower beds with several enormous oaks that looked centuries old. The fog was beginning to break up and patches of blue sky could be seen.

The library had bookcases on three of the four walls, stuffed to overflowing. There were piles of books and papers on every horizontal surface, including stacks of them on the carpet. There was an old desk in front of the window, paper cascading across the scarred surface like drifts of snow. Finn immediately felt at home; her father's study had looked a lot like this.

There were two leather armchairs in front of the desk. The old man unceremoniously swept the stacks of books and papers off them and gestured for Finn and Billy to sit down. "Back in a jif," the old man said and disappeared.

"Nice old sort," said Billy, looking around the warm, chaotic room.

"According to my information he locked a man into a cabin on a burning ship in the Caribbean. He was an assassin for Israeli intelligence."

"Where do you manage to find these people?" Billy said. "He certainly had me fooled."

A few minutes later the old man appeared with a tray of tea things, including a small plate piled high with an assortment of fancy cookies. He put the tray down on the desk, fixed the tea according to their various preferences, then plucked a bourbon crème biscuit off the plate, sat down in the chair on the far side of the desk, dipped his cookie briefly into his teacup and took a soggy bite.

"Teeth aren't what they used to be," he explained, munching happily. He took a sip of his tea, made a contented sound of appreciation, and sat back against the creaking old leather of his chair. "If you know me as Martin Kerzner then you must have known Abramo Vergadora at one time or another."

Vergadora was an Italian historian Finn had met two years before while investigating the Lost Legion of Luciferus Africanus and the disappearance of the so-called Lucifer Gospel.

"Yes, briefly," answered Finn.

"If memory serves, Miss Ryan, you were involved in his murder."

"I was with him shortly before he was killed, yes," she answered tightly.

"In the end responsibility for his death was laid at the feet of *Terza Positione*, the Third Position, a radical terrorist cell in Italy," said the old man.

"You're well-informed for a retired theology teacher," said Finn.

"Have you ever heard of an organization called P-Two, also Italian?"

"No."

"It stands for *Propaganda Due*. It was a secret society allied with the Vatican with the intent of fighting Communism by the creation of a paramilitary 'authoritarian' democracy in Italy. At one time they had infiltrated every level of Italian society, from university professors and policemen to the prime minster himself. *Terza Positione* was one of its front groups. P-Two was supposedly outlawed after its discovery during the Vatican bank scandal in 1981 and dissolved."

"You're saying it wasn't?"

"Yes. It simply reinvented itself under another name."

"*Cavallo Nero*, the Order of the Black Knights," said Billy.

"Quite right, Lord Pilgrim," the old man answered.

Billy looked stunned. "You know who I am?"

"Certainly, and Miss Ryan as well. I am old, my lord, but I am not a fool. My friends in Lausanne gave me ample warning, not to mention the fact that both of you were all over the news last year after your somewhat dramatic escapades in the South China Sea."

"I'd prefer it if you just called me Billy."

"Not William?"

"William was my father. Billy is better."

"As you wish."

"*Cavallo Nero*," reminded Finn. "Friar Bartolome de las Casas."

"Ah, yes," murmured the old man. "The Aztec Heresy of Hernán Cortéz. And the fate of the *Nuestra Señora de las Angustias* off Key West, Florida."

"From which virtually all the treasure was recovered the following year, 1522, and Bartolome de las Casas rescued. That much was in the records in Seville," said Billy.

The old man laughed and chose another biscuit. "Seville. The Archives of Broken Dreams. A thousand plans hatched, ten thousand treasure maps described. Did you know that Tomás de Torquemada, the first Grand Inquisitor, held the original tribunal of the Spanish Inquisition in the very building that houses the Archives of the Indies today? If those walls could speak you'd hear nothing but the screams of the damned."

"I still don't see the connection to this *Cavallo Nero* group," said Finn.

"P-Two was effectively a continuation of the Inquisition—the Vatican Inquisition—all of it, not just the Spanish directorate. Their job then, as now, was to root out the enemies of the Holy Church and deal with them. Often violently. At some level they had to be at arm's length from the Vatican itself, so they invested special powers in the Dominican order to do so. The so-called Hounds of God—*Domine Canis*, an old joke, I'm afraid. Their job was to find the heretics. The particularly powerful and important ones like Hernán Cortéz were handled by an even more secret group within the Dominicans—the *Cavallo Nero*. The Black Knights. Effectively they were the Vatican's hit men." He paused. "They still are."

"Cortéz was a heretic?"

"Hernán Cortéz was extremely wealthy by the time he'd finished with Mexico. And he wasn't leaving, which worried the governor of Cuba at the time, Don Diego Velázquez. Somehow he discovered that Cortéz had hidden a vast fortune from the court of the king and he had proof."

"The Codex."

"Yes." The old man nodded. "A complete history, including precise directions to the secret hoard, a virtual city of gold in the Yucatán jungle."

"What happened to the Codex?" Billy asked.

"Bartolome de las Casas was taking it to the Vatican. It was lost aboard the *Nuestra Señora de las Angustias*. Destroyed in the wreck."

"But the story doesn't end there, does it?" Finn said.

"Stories like that never do. That's how they become mysteries and legends."

"How does it end?"

"With a question mark"—the old man smiled—"and rumors."

"What kind of rumors?" Finn asked.

"Rumors that Don Diego Velázquez, the governor of Cuba and Cortéz's sworn enemy, was no fool. He had a copy of the Codex made and sent it off on another ship, the *San Anton*, a *nau*, or *caravella*, a much smaller ship than the treasure galleons. Some were less than a hundred tons. They were fast, mostly used to carry important passengers or documents."

"Like the copy of the Codex," said Billy.

"Umm." The old man nodded. "Like the Codex."

"What happened to her?" Finn said.

"She sank in the same hurricane as the *Nuestra Señora de las Angustias*," said the old man. He poured himself another cup of tea and took a third biscuit from the plate.

"Where?" Billy asked.

"Ah," said the old man, eyes twinkling behind his candy-colored spectacles. "Now that's an entirely different story."

"One you're willing to tell us?" Finn asked quietly.

"I'd be happy to tell you if I knew, but that sort of thing is well outside my present mandate."

"Mandate?" Billy said. "Odd word."

"Have you ever heard of an organization called the Vatican Watch?"

"Good Lord, not another secret society!" Billy laughed.

The old man smiled. "Nothing secret about it at all, although we don't advertise our existence very strenuously."

"What is Vatican Watch?" Finn asked.

"An association of concerned Catholics, lay members as well as those like myself, people with a religious vocation. We monitor the activities of certain groups within the Holy See. Discreetly. One would assume that the Vatican of all places could police its own activities, but events of the last hundred years or so have sadly confounded that hypothesis."

"*Quis custodiet ipsos custodes?*" Billy nodded.

"The benefits of a classical education, I see," said the old man.

"Who shall watch the watchers?" translated Finn. "You learn a few things in public school as well."

"Quite so," the old man said. "You're quite right to chide me. I've become something of a snob in my old age." He dipped his cookie again. "Plato, and later Juvenal, were perfectly correct. The watchers are not capable of watching themselves since any position is corruptible. Thus, the monitoring must fall to those

64

outside the organization being monitored. That is the origins of Vatican Watch."

"And Vatican Watch has been monitoring *Cavallo Nero?*"

"Yes. For many years."

"What does any of this have to do with Cortéz and the Codex?" Finn asked, her tone a little frustrated.

"Nothing directly," said the old man. "But *Cavallo Nero* has made a number of somewhat disreputable alliances over the years to further their cause."

"What sort of alliances?" Billy asked.

"Dangerous ones," said the old man. "It is not so much the Codex but where the Codex leads that is important. Equally, it is the people along the way to that destination who we find disturbing."

"Who?" Finn asked bluntly.

"It is not my place to say. In fact, if anything, my purpose is to warn you against pursuing this matter any further."

"And if we decide not to heed your warning?"

"Then go with God," said the old man. "But before that I suggest you visit a friend of mine."

"Who?"

"His name is Pierre Jumaire. He lives in Paris. He operates a bookstore on the rue de la Huchette. Perhaps he can guide you better than I."

7

Rue de la Huchette is a short narrow street on the Left Bank of the Seine one block in from the river and the Quai St. Michel. The street runs between rue de Petit Pont on the east and Boulevard St. Michel on the west. "Huchette" is probably an archaic bastardization of the word "hachette," or "hatchet," which stands to reason since the street was once predominantly occupied by charcoal burners, who must have chopped a great deal of the hardwood from the local forests that grew in what was at one time the outskirts of Paris.

For most of the twentieth century rue de la Huchette was an eclectic mix of cafés, small hotels, and neighborhood shops that ranged from Le Garage de Terreur to a pawnshop named Aux Temps Dificiles, and a brothel called Le Panier Fleuri. It formed the backdrop for dozens of movies, and by the fifties it had been made famous in at least two books, *The Last Time I Saw Paris* and *Springtime in Paris.*

By the beginning of the twenty-first century all that had changed. Mado, Daisy, Consuelo, and Amandine, once the favorites at Le Panier Fleuri, were all great-grandmothers, and Monge the horse butcher was long dead, as was his trade. L'Oursin, the man who'd once sold chestnuts outside the Pharmacie Rabat at the corner of the narrow alley romantically known as rue de Chat Qui Peche—Street of the Fishing Cat—vanished the day Kennedy was shot and was never heard from again. The street was now filled with Greek restaurants offering cheap plates for smashing, overpriced boutiques selling questionable name brands, and trendy bed-and-breakfasts for trendy tourists. The last remnant of what had once been the essence of Hemingway and Fitzgerald's Left Bank was Librarie Pierre Jumaire, a dusty little bookshop on the corner at rue de Petit Pont.

The shop was a classic: dark, dusty shelves stuck here and there wherever there was room, books in piles everywhere, crammed in willynilly with little regard for price or age, the popular beside the obscure, the sublime sharing space with the profane, and all of it smelling faintly of mildew, ink, and binding glue.

Jumaire himself was equally an archetype: he was squat, old, his white hair a halolike memory on the edges of a freckled skull; he wore thick bifocals and a black suit with a green bow tie on the worn collar of his wrinkled white shirt. There were two heavy briarwood canes beside his high stool behind the counter in the front where he held court, always with a fat yellow Boyard cigarette dangling between his thin lips and poking out of his bushy white beard, the mustache the color of nicotine, his right eye in a permanent squint where the acrid smoke wound its way up beneath the lenses of his spectacles.

Librarie Pierre Jumaire had always specialized in nautical books, and the very tops of the bookcases were decorated with ships in bottles, bits of carved ivory, and a collection of brass navigation instruments, none of which had felt the touch of a duster for more than half a century. On the rare occasions that Jumaire left the shop, he inevitably wore an ancient peaked officer's cap and a dark blue peacoat that could easily have been worn by Melville's Ishmael in *Moby-Dick*.

As Finn and Billy entered the store, Jumaire was arguing with a customer in a loud voice and waving his arms to illustrate his point. The customer eventually slapped several bills down on the counter, picked up his purchase, and left in a huff, brushing past them and banging the door hard enough to make the little dangling bell at the lintel ring angrily.

"Idiot!" Jumaire said to no one in particular.

"Trying to bargain?" Billy asked, smiling.

"Ach!" Jumaire answered. "The price is written on the flyleaf of every volume. This is not some bazaar in the souk at Marrakech. Would they argue over the price of a Royale with cheese at McDonald's? I think not!" Finn burst out laughing. Jumaire eyed her severely. "You are very pretty, my dear, and I have a weakness for women with red hair, but I am quite serious. The fools try my patience endlessly. Would you barter at Hermes or Christian Dior? No again, of course you would not! They throw you out on your pretty little ear. Faugh!"

"Sorry," said Finn.

"Beautiful women should never apologize," answered Jumaire, eyes twinkling behind his glasses.

"Martin Kerzner sent us," said Billy.

"Really," said Jumaire.

"Yes."

"He said you could help us."

"Will and can are two entirely different words."

"We understand that," said Finn.

"We're trying to find out what happened to the *San Anton*," said Billy.

"She sank in a storm," answered Jumaire.

"But where?"

"Ah," said Jumaire. "As Long John Silver would say, 'there's the rub.'"

"We thought you could help," said Finn.

"Why should I?"

"Because *Cavallo Nero* is trying to find out as well," said Billy.

"Ah," said Jumaire again. "The fiends from the Vatican. The new great Satan for thriller writers."

"You think they're a fiction?"

"No, of course not. They're genuine enough, but they have nothing really to do with the Vatican. There is no sinister conspiracy of albino men of the cloth protecting the secrets of the new millennium via strange messages embedded in the streets of Paris or old paintings. The only thing embedded in the streets of Paris is used bubble gum. It is as it ever was: it is all about money. The Inquisition was about greed and power. It still is."

"Will you help us?" Finn said bluntly.

"Certainly," said Jumaire with a shrug. "Why not?"

"That was easy enough," said Finn. "Why the sudden trust?"

"Kerzner told you we were coming," said Billy, suddenly understanding. "He called to warn you."

"Of course. He described Miss Ryan perfectly."

The old man struggled to his feet, balancing himself on his canes. "Turn the sign on the door, throw the bolt, and pull down the blind," he instructed Billy. The reverse of the OPEN sign read *Entrailles pas Fiables*: uncertain bowels. "It covers a multitude of situations and rarely invites questions," explained Jumaire. He came out from behind the counter and headed through the stacks. "Follow me, if you please. I have rooms in the back. I'll make coffee for us."

Max Kessler sat in Jack Kennedy's bomb shelter and examined the file he had assembled on Harrison Noble and his father. It made interesting reading. Noble

Pharmaceuticals had begun as a family business almost a hundred years before, trafficking in patent medicines of all kinds but specializing in nostrums, pills, powders, and tonics, a number of them containing opium derivatives, several based on cocaine and one extremely popular concoction used for distress related to "a particular periodic occurrence" named Lady Helen's Tonic, which contained a healthy dose of heroin. Over the decades Noble Pharmaceuticals added to its fortunes, expanding into a variety of over-the-counter products but maintaining a solid base in patent medicine of all kinds, especially its flagship product, Noble's Mixture, a cure-all that was still being sold well into the fifties. In 1960 Conrad Noble, the family patriarch, died, and James Jonas Noble took over. His first act was to change the names of almost all their products. Thus, Noble's Mixture became Nomix, Grady's Hair Tonic became Brillamine, and Noble's Liver Pills became Heparine. Under James Noble's guidance the company slowly phased out the old quack items and began the manufacture of generic prescription drugs, carefully watching the growth of antipsychotics and antidepressants based on the ever-expanding volume of new diseases being listed in the *Diagnostic and Statistical Manual of Mental Disorders*, generally referred to as the DSM and presently in its fourth incarnation, DSM-IV, in which "shyness" had become something called Social Anxiety Disorder, or SAD.

Every time a new DSM mentioned a new disease, Noble found a drug for it or adapted someone else's. Prozac and Paxil became Danex, Zoloft became Antipan, and Celexa became Cytoloft. A drug by any other name made billions. By the year 2000 Noble Pharmaceuticals was the eighth largest drug manufacturer in the world, and their motto, "We Feel Your Pain," had been adopted by *Late Night with David Letterman* and spoofed regularly on *Saturday Night Live*. The humorless lawyers for Noble Pharmaceuticals assured James Noble that he had grounds for a lawsuit, but the CEO told them not to be silly, it was free advertising on an enormous scale.

Harrison Noble, James Noble's only child, was only a faint reflection of his father, and some of the gossip columnists said the only things he'd inherited from his father were a strong chin and a weakness for blondes. A student at Yale and a member of Skull and Bones only because of his father, Harrison Noble had no particular interests except spending his trust fund and seeing how many debutantes he could sleep with, until he started sleeping with the daughter of the president of the United States and managed to get her pregnant. The silencing of the scandal of both the pregnancy and its termination led to an ultimatum from his father about making something of himself, which in turn resulted in Noble Ventures, ostensibly an oceanographic foundation funded by Noble Pharmaceuticals but really nothing more than an excuse to provide a platform for a series of ill-advised treasure-hunting expeditions and a way to indulge Harrison Noble's passion for scuba diving and island hopping through the Caribbean. It also managed to fulfill his father's desire for keeping his son out of dangerous political bedrooms. The connection between the younger Noble and a drug czar like Angel Guzman led Max Kessler's analytical intellect down a number of intriguing avenues and bore closer attention, especially if, as Max Kessler surmised, Harrison Noble was acting for his father. Like the taped door at the Watergate Hotel that led to Nixon's resignation, Max knew the tip of an iceberg when he saw it.

8

Pierre Jumaire poured coffee and set out a plate of petit fours in his simple kitchen, then sat down with Finn and Billy. "I'm still not sure of the importance of the Codex," said Billy.

"Beyond its intrinsic value as a historical document, the Cortéz Codex was proof of Cortéz's treason. He was hiding a vast treasure from King Charles. In those days the monarchy received a *quinto*, one-fifth of any plunder from any expedition to the New World. By that time Cortéz himself was so powerful that the only way to deal with him was by having him excommunicated by the Inquisition, in which case all his lands and treasures would be forfeit to the Church, which would in turn pass on an agreed-upon proportion to the crown. It was exactly the kind of thing the Nazis did to the Jews in the thirties and Roosevelt did to the interned Japanese after Pearl Harbor. Government-sanctioned theft, all neat and tidy and done according to the laws of the day."

"Follow the money," murmured Finn.

"Generally a wise course to follow as a historian," said Jumaire. He sipped his coffee, then lit another of his foul-smelling cigarettes.

"Why would anyone be interested in the Codex now?" Finn asked.

"Because it is a treasure map, of course," answered the bookseller. "You're proof of its interest yourself."

"I don't buy that," answered Finn. "You and your friend Brother Kerzner haven't been hanging around on the off chance that someone's going to come looking for a five-hundred-year-old scrap of parchment."

"It's actually tree bark," said the bookseller mildly.

"Called *amatl*. Made from a fig tree, usually *Ficus padifolia*," she answered just as mildly. "As I said, a public education from Ohio can be quite good."

"Touché," Jumaire said and laughed. "I apologize."

"Apology accepted," said Finn. "But you still haven't answered my question."

"*Tue-mouches*," said Jumaire.

"Flypaper," translated Billy.

"I don't get it," said Finn.

"A lure," explained the old man. "We are aware of the interest *Cavallo Nero* has in such things. The more we know of their activities, the better."

"Forewarned is forearmed," said Billy.

"Something like that."

"And has somebody from the Black Knights been sniffing around?" Finn asked.

"Let's just say you're not alone in your interest," said the old man coyly.

"You're making this sound like a dangerous proposition," said Billy.

"*Cavallo Nero* has been known to be somewhat extreme in its methods," agreed Jumaire.

"So you're warning us off?"

"No, merely informing you of the reality of the situation. *Cavallo Nero* is of the opinion that they are sanctioned by God Himself." Jumaire glanced at Finn with a smile. "Or Herself. Thus anything they do can be justified. The Inquisition can do no wrong since they are in fact the arbiters of what is right. An extension of Papal infallibility. Very convenient."

"Do you know where the *San Anton* sank?" Finn asked bluntly. "I want to know what all the fuss is about."

"So be it." The old man paused. "By most estimations it sank off Key West, Cayo Hueso as it was known then, the Island of Bones. In fact, the likelihood is that it managed to turn north and run before the hurricane for some time before it sank."

"Which was where?"

"The North Cape of Bimini Island, fifty miles off Miami." He smiled, this time unpleasantly. "Coincidentally, less than a thousand yards from the Bimini Road."

"The Bimini Road?" Billy frowned.

"Edgar Cayce. Atlantis." Finn sighed. "Woo-woo territory."

"Very impressive," said Jumaire.

"That Ohio-public-school-education-thing again," said Finn.

"You can't beat it."

"Woo-woo?" Billy asked.

There was no direct flight from Paris, so Finn and Billy headed back to London through the Chunnel, caught a BA jumbo out of Heathrow, and then spent ten hours and four time zones droning down the entire length of the North Atlantic Ocean eating stale food on plastic trays and alternately listening to Bruce Springsteen and watching Bruce Willis save the world again, this time without any hair at all. Columbus had a hard time getting to the Caribbean, but by the time Finn arrived in Nassau she was pretty sure she'd rather have sailed on the *Santa Maria* than flown on British Airways.

They arrived, bleary-eyed and yawning, at Lynden Pindling International Airport at ten in the morning local time. After going through customs they walked into the scruffy waiting room and headed for the doors. A pair of workmen were shifting a big Kalik Beer display while an airport janitor dusted off a huge fading cardboard effigy of Daniel Craig as James Bond that had been there since the movie opened and refused to leave. Some joker had

78

scribbled "mashup boy" across the figure's chest in marker and added a Hitler mustache to 007's upper lip. The superspy wound up looking like a very stern version of Charlie Chaplin with a gun.

They stepped out into the bright hot sun in front of the airport. The air was like a physical blow and Finn dragged in a lungful of the island scent; a mingling of rotting vegetation, exotic perfumes, and the salt of the surrounding sea. As promised, Sidney Poitier was there to meet them in his battered old Toyota taxi.

"Good mornin', good mornin', how are you this mornin'?" The old man shook his head. "This what worl' travelin' does for you then I want no part of it," continued Sidney, eyeing Finn and Billy as they dragged themselves into the old car. "You look like somethin' unhappy the kitty-cat put in the sandbox." He peered at them in the rearview mirror. "You going to the boat?"

"Please," said Finn, letting her head fall back against the seat. Sidney industriously hammered the car into gear and jerked away from the curb. The old man wrestled the rattling car around Killarney Lake, then brought it staggering down John F. Kennedy Drive to West Bay Street and the string of aging hotels that stood in a long, well-manicured row along Cable Beach, the unbelievably turquoise ocean stretching out to the horizon beyond.

They reached the outskirts of Nassau ten minutes later, which was like coming in the back door of any small town in the Caribbean: pastel-colored buildings surrounded by crumbling stucco walls topped with razor wire, classic, old-fashioned resort hotels on the beach side of the street, and potholes everywhere. They passed a few of the pint-sized, privately owned jitney buses ferrying tourists into town from Cable Beach, tumbling out rake-and-scrape and goombay music from blaring loudspeakers set over the windshields. Through breaks between the buildings and the palms, they saw half a dozen overweight-looking cruise ships, sparkling white except for the crimson blot of the old *Big Red Boat*, once the Disney flagship but now owned by an obscure cartel of Spanish businessmen.

Poitier guided the rattletrap taxi through a quick set of left and right turns, finally coming out onto Bay Street again, now one way with all the traffic pointing east toward the bridge to Paradise Island and the Atlantis resort with its enormous aquarium and even larger casinos. Until the building of Atlantis, Bay Street had been the relatively civilized two-way main thoroughfare of Nassau, but the one-way change had turned traffic into a chaotic choked parade of taxis, jitney buses, and private cars turning up and down narrow side streets in an almost impossible effort to go in any other direction but east, through the center of town.

Poitier managed to get them out of the morning rush-hour hell past the banks and souvenir shops that lined both sides of Bay Street, past the government buildings and the brooding, funereal statue of Queen Victoria, finally heading down to the commercial docks and warehouses at the foot of Armstrong Street, just before the bridge to Atlantis.

Back down Bay Street at the Prince George Wharf, where the cruise ships docked, there was everything from a marketplace for stuffed barracuda heads, polished conch shells, and straw hats to half-naked men who'd behead a coconut for you with a single swipe of their machetes and twelve-year-old girls who'd give you cornrows for a dollar a plait. At the Armstrong wharf there was an old fireboat, a few conch-fishing trawlers, a couple of bottled-water barges from Miami, and two bottom-of-the-barrel deep-sea charters, wooden boats from the fifties, paint peeling, teak decks bleached bone white after half a century of salt and sun.

And then there was the *Hispaniola*. They'd argued about the name for weeks, trying out everything from the *Gold Bug* to the *Dawn Treader*—and every other fictional ship name in between from the *Witch of Endor* to the *Orca*, from *Jaws*. In the end the only one they could agree on was *Hispaniola*, the ship that had taken Jim Hawkins and Long John Silver to Treasure Island, although, according to Billy, Robert Louis Stevenson's nephew had unilaterally decreed that his uncle should not put any girls into the story, which Finn resented, just a little.

The *Hispaniola* had a history older than either Finn or Billy. Dutch-built by J. T. Smith & Zone in 1962 for a British owner and originally named *M.V. Severn*, the *Hispaniola* was a 175-foot-long oceangoing tug that spent most of its early working life dragging oil rigs around the North Sea. She had been bought and sold several times since but had been rescued from the scrap yard by their lawyer, friend, and junior partner, Guido Derlagen, the stuffy Amsterdamer who'd thrown off his bureaucratic ways and now did all their legal work for them wearing unbelievably wild Tommy Bahamas tropical shirts and sunbathing on the bridge deck. Guido, who managed the incredible wealth they'd discovered in the secret room of the ancient house Billy and Finn had inherited on the Herengracht canal, got a respectable deal on the thirty-five-year-old tug, and eighteen months later it was reborn at Scheldepoort in Flushing as a free-ranging explorer yacht that could take its new owners around the world and back again, her twin diesels cruising at a respectable twelve knots through any seas you could throw at her. The only problem with the ship was that the engines never gave Run-Run McSeveney, their half-Scot, half-Chinese engineer, any trouble at all, a fact that made him even more cranky than usual. Of the original crew of the old *Batavia Queen*, the rusting freighter they'd lost during a China Sea typhoon two years before, McSeveney, Briney Hanson, the master, and Eli Santoro, the eye-patch-wearing thirty-year-old ex-U.S. Navy first officer, were all that was left, but after her refit the *Hispaniola* had been equipped with every piece of automated marine equipment you could think of, and under ordinary circumstances she was relatively easy to operate. With the addition of Lloyd Terco, an old Bahamian friend, as cook and able seaman, the seven-person crew was complete.

"Home again, home again," said Sidney, pulling the Toyota to a shuddering stop on the pier. Beside them, the black-hulled *Hispaniola* loomed over them, her superstructure blinding white. A warehouse beside them breathed rotten fruit. The harbor smelled of diesel oil and dead fish. On the tin roof of the warehouse you could still read the old painted slogan used by the tourist authority, faded away almost to nothing: "It's Better in the Bahamas."

Finn and Billy climbed out of the taxi and stretched. Under a makeshift awning set up above the bridge deck, Guido waved a cheerful welcome, his tanned bald head covered by a raffia Shady Brady fedora, his torso covered by a loose floral-print shirt.

"*Feestelijk inhalen!*" Guido called out enthusiastically.

A split second later Run-Run McSeveney pushed out through the chart room door directly below Guido's perch and glared up at him. "Speak English, ya bluidy tulip seller! I've told ye that a hunnert times. This is one of Her Majesty's colonies and ye'll speak her tongue when ye're here, mind!"

"*Loop naar de hel, eikel.*" Guido laughed.

"What did he say?" Billy asked.

"I think *eikel* means 'dickhead,'" said Finn. "I don't know about the rest of it."

They took their bags out of the Toyota and Sidney drove off. The two young people climbed up the companionway and stepped onto the main deck. Everything looked exactly the way they'd left it. Briney Hanson, the *Hispaniola* 's master, came down from the deck above and they headed into the main lounge amidships. Lloyd Terco appeared, stringy as ever wearing flip-flops and one of his signature wife-beater undershirts. He gave the two a happy smile, welcomed them back, and took their bags down to their cabins.

The lounge was fitted with built-in couches, a few old leather chairs, and had a Ping-Pong table at one end and a vintage Bally pinball machine and a soft-drink machine at the other. On Billy's standing order the soft-drink machine only dispensed cans of Kalik beer.

Hanson guided them to a pair of comfortable club chairs, then sprawled on one of the couches and lit one of his clove-scented cigarettes. The deeply tanned, dark-haired, muscular-looking Dane eyed them curiously.

"Your e-mail was pretty vague. Did you find out anything?"

"The Bimini Road," said Billy Pilgrim. He nodded toward Finn. "Our fearless leader is about to take us into the realm of the supernatural."

"You're kidding," sighed Hanson.

"Atlantis, actually," Billy said and laughed. "Which apparently was located about a hundred miles east of Walt Disney World."

"It figures," said Hanson, sighing again, with feeling.

9

The old Foxtrot submarine surfaced in the predawn darkness, the jungle coastline of the Yucatán Peninsula a darker shadow on the nighttime horizon barely a mile away. Water streamed from the rounded shoulders of her pale sleek hull as it heaved itself into the air. Bright foam swirled around the conning tower as it broke through the turquoise swell, leaving a phosphorescent scar in the troubled water.

Enrico Ramirez, Arkady Cruz's second in command, knocked on the bulkhead beside the curtain over the entrance to the small niche that passed for a cabin on board the *Babaloo*. Cruz came awake almost instantly.

"Yes?"

"We're here."

What time is it?"

"O five hundred."

"How much under the keel?"

"Sixty fathoms, sir."

"All right." Cruz slipped out of the built-in bunk fully clothed and pulled open the curtain. Ramirez, stoop-shouldered with his gray hair buzzed short like a convict, stood calmly, holding a steaming mug in one hand. He handed the mug to his captain. Cruz accepted it gratefully and took a long swallow of the thick, sweet *cafecito*. Cruz smiled. He commanded the only submarine in the world that had its own espresso machine.

"Any sign of the Mexican?"

"Not yet."

"This isn't my favorite part of the game," said Cruz.

"No, sir."

Cruz emptied the mug and handed it back to Ramirez.

"Let's go."

He heaved himself up off the bunk, grabbed his peaked cap off the hook on the bulkhead, and jammed it down on his head. He followed Ramirez down the claustrophobic corridor that ran the length of the old boat, ducking as he pulled himself through the narrow bulkhead doors. He reached the control room, nodded to the few officers of the watch, then went after Ramirez up the ladder through the conning tower to the bridge lookout.

"Why do submarines always smell like your feet, Ramirez?" Cruz asked, grinning and breathing in the sea air.

"My feet smell like the revolution, Capitaine. It is a mark of patriotism to have feet that smell like mine. Che himself said so."

"You knew Guevara then?" Cruz answered, continuing the old joke.

"I washed his feet, Capitaine. I have endeavored to make my own smell exactly as his did."

"Good for you, Ramirez. Fidel would be proud."

"I thought the Great One had been stuffed and mounted over his own mantel," said Ramirez.

"Don't believe everything his brother Raul tells you, Ramirez."

"No, sir."

"Hand me my glasses."

"Yes, sir." He handed Cruz a pair of Russian-made Baigish night-vision binoculars. The captain took them and scanned the water between the waiting submarine and the shore. Five minutes passed. It was definitely getting lighter. Cruz swore. If the crazy bastard thought he'd wait until broad daylight he had another thing coming.

"Time?"

"O five fifteen."

"*Deirymo*," muttered Cruz in Russian

"*Cono*," agreed Ramirez in Spanish.

"There he is," said Arkady Cruz, pointing.

"Asshole," said Ramirez in perfect, unaccented English.

The boat was a Canadian Grand Marine inflatable S650, twenty-one feet long and overpowered beyond specifications with two-hundred-and-fifty horsepower

Evinrudes capable of ripping the no-draft boat through the water at speeds in excess of seventy miles per hour. The boat had zero radar reflectivity and a fourteen-hundred-kilo cargo capacity. There was a single .50-caliber machine gun mounted in the bow. Angel Guzman had more than a score of the big rubber boats hidden in the mangroves along the coast from Isla Mojeres all the way down to Chetumal and the border of Belize. Like the *Babaloo*, the boat racing toward them out of the rising darkness was colored pale blue and was almost invisible on the water. Each one was equipped with two camouflage awnings made out of heavy netting, one for the open ocean and one for the jungle swamps. Each carried enough fuel to give the boats almost a five-hundred-mile range.

The boat turned harshly, throwing up a rooster tail of spray, and abruptly stopped beside the low-riding hull of the submarine. The machine gun in the bow was unmanned. There was only one person in the boat: a uniformed man at the wheel. The uniform was standard jungle camouflage, fatigues neatly pushed into combat boots, a canvas-holstered sidearm on the hip. The only thing out of the ordinary was the bloodred beret the man wore, the mark of an officer in the army of Angel Guzman, an *Angelista*, as the American DEA referred to them.

"Time to go," said Arkady. Ramirez nodded. "Take her down to the bottom and keep her there. Unless Signor Guzman decides to boil me in a pot for his breakfast or carve my heart out as a sacrifice to one of his gods, I should be back by nightfall. Keep a candle burning in the window."

"It shall be done, master," said Ramirez, his expression bland. "Although I fear it will get damp."

"You're such a joker, Rico, a regular Billy Crystal," said Arkady Cruz, who was a fan, particularly of both *City Slickers* as well as *The Princess Bride*.

"Geraldo Seinfeld," said Ramirez, who had all nine seasons on a bootleg set from China.

Cruz gave his friend a quick salute then slid down inside the conning tower ladder to the bridge deck. He popped open a watertight bulkhead door at the foot of the conning tower, then stepped out onto the ribbed, slightly pitching deck. He dogged down the door behind him, crossed the deck, and dropped down into the inflatable, taking a seat in the stern. A few seconds later the huge twin outboards roared into life and the rubber boat spun around and headed toward the shore. Behind them the *Babaloo* blew her main ballast tanks with a hissing roar and sank beneath the waters once again, disappearing from view just as the first rays of the rising sun came arrowing out of the east across the wide blue sea.

While Briney Hanson guided the *Hispaniola* out of Nassau Harbour past Montagu Beach and turned the big tug into Hanover Sound, the rest of the crew gathered in the Main Salon.

"What exactly is the Bimini Road?" Eli Santoro asked. He was in Johnny Depp mode today, wearing a ragged pair of cutoffs, a black skull-and-bones T-shirt, a bandanna over his dark hair, and his leather eye patch. He'd lost the eye in a barbecuing accident while serving with the U.S. Navy in Guam, and the deficient sight had lost him his commission and his future. Rather than take a desk job in the navy he'd chosen the life of a crew bum and wound up as Briney Hanson's first officer on the old *Batavia Queen*. The rusted-out hulk of a freighter had gone aground in the middle of a China Sea typhoon, and when the smoke cleared and Finn and Billy decided to start their Treasure Seekers venture, he and Briney had been the first to sign on as crew.

"Bimini Road is a rock formation off the island of North Bimini," said Guido Derlagen. As well as being the group's maritime lawyer, cook's assistant, and the only one on board who knew anything about computers, the Dutchman had also become their unofficial researcher. "It is about half a mile long at a depth of thirty feet. Generally it can only be seen from the air. It was discovered by a pilot in 1969, which conforms to the prediction made by the American clairvoyant Edgar Cayce in 1938."

Eli shook his head in awe. "You're spooky, Guido—you know that?"

"*Dankzegging*." The big skin-headed Netherlander smiled with a little bow. "You would like me to continue, yes?"

"Yes," said Finn.

"*Dankzegging*," Guido repeated, and went on. "Although it is said by most geologists that it is a natural formation, these people following the predictions of Mr. Cayce are sure it is a road."

"Anybody ever find anything other than this so-called road?" Eli asked from the couch. "Any other evidence?"

"Alas, not," said Guido.

"Where exactly is this place?"

"Half a mile off North Bimini Island off Paradise Point," put in Finn. "It's a popular dive site for tourists. Glass-bottom boats, that kind of thing."

"Pardon me for asking," said Run-Run McSeveney, his small face twisting into a scowl, "but it was my impression this wee venture was to find bits of gold and other valuable trinkets. Doubloons and pieces of eight and the like. What do these bluidy stones have to do with that, might I inquire?" As always, the thick Glasgow brogue coming from the definitely Chinese face was enough to make Finn smile.

"There've been some recent theories that the Bimini Road might be the remains of an offshore coffer dam or dry dock. The kind of thing that might have been used in an early attempt to salvage or refloat a sunken ship."

"Thirty feet's not a lot of water," said Billy. "They raised the Tudor ship *Mary Rose* from forty feet below the Solent. The technology for that sort of dry dock is hundreds of years old."

"There'd have to be something valuable aboard for it to have been worthwhile," said Finn.

"Doubloons and the like," said Run-Run, licking his lips, his black eyes glinting.

"We think it may be the site of an attempt to refloat a ship called the *San Anton*, a Spanish ship from the sixteenth century."

"A treasure ship?" Run-Run asked.

"A small trader, a dispatch ship," answered Billy. "But a ship with a secret all its own."

"Surely that area's been gone over with a fine-tooth comb by now," said Eli.

"Probably," agreed Finn. "But by people looking for big treasure galleons, not smaller ships. The *San Anton* was less than a hundred tons. Even with side-scanning radar and all the newest bells and whistles it would be hard to spot."

"So what gives us the advantage?" Eli asked.

Billy smiled. "We know exactly where to look."

James Jonas Noble, head of Noble Pharmaceuticals, sipped a Grant's Ale Cask scotch and looked out the porthole as the Cessna Mustang business jet ripped up into the pale blue sky over Miami and headed due east. Across from him, in another one of the cream-colored leather club seats, his son, Harrison, gripped his glass of diet Coke and sucked on the half lemon slice it came with. He hated flying and his old man knew it, which was why they were making the fifteen-minute flight to their private estate on Cat Cay rather than the two-hour trip in the *Noble Dancer*, the company boat they kept at the house on Fisher Island just off South Beach.

"They found it?" Harrison Noble said to his father, talking around the lemon slice.

"So I'm told."

"On Bimini?"

"Offshore. Somehow they managed to find the exact location," said the gray-haired man across from him.

"What are we going to do now?"

"Deal with it. Negotiations have reached a critical phase with our friend in Mexico." He looked toward the closed door leading to the cockpit. He lowered his voice a little. "We can't let anything stand in our way. The second-quarter earnings aren't what I expected."

"What about the new drug?"

"I can't announce it before the Mexican deal is completed, and that means getting this Englishman and his little American girlfriend out of the way. We have to seal things up. Tight." The older man sipped his drink.

The plane hit a patch of turbulence and Harrison Noble gripped his diet Coke even harder.

"I won't let you down, Dad."

"You're damn right you won't," his father snapped. "If you screw this up we're both dead and don't you forget it."

The biz jet flew on.

Pierre Jumaire looked down the dusty aisle and frowned. It was getting late, dusk turning the street outside into gloomy puddles of shadow between the streetlamps. He wanted to close up. Only one customer remained, a man in his thirties, thin with glasses and a studious expression. He was wearing a black suit that was frayed at the trouser cuffs. He'd been reading the same volume for the last ten minutes. He didn't look like a buyer. Maybe a book thief. The book he was reading was a first edition of Voltaire's *Lettres philosophiques sur les Anglais* in a nice leather binding.

"Monsieur," he said loudly, "this is not a lending library. It is a bookstore. I wish to close. Buy if you will, but whatever you do, please do it quickly."

The man looked up and smiled pleasantly, clearly not taking offense at the old man's tone. He closed the book carefully and came up the aisle. A buyer after all. Appearances could be deceiving.

"I like Voltaire," said the man.

"So do I," replied Jumaire. "I believe that particular volume is two hundred and fifty Euros."

"I know many books which have bored their readers, but I know of none which has done real evil," the man answered.

"The multitude of books is making us ignorant," responded Jumaire. "We have now proved that we can both quote Voltaire. The price, however, is still two hundred and fifty Euros."

"You won't take anything less?" the man asked.

"This is not the Marche aux puces, monsieur," Jumaire responded with a sigh. "I never bargain."

"You do today." The man reached into the inside pocket of his jacket and pulled out a Russian-made Stechkin Automatic Pistol. He shot Jumaire in the face. It made a cracking sound like a balloon bursting. Jumaire slipped behind the counter. The man put the weapon back into the inside pocket of his jacket and walked out of the store, taking the copy of Voltaire with him.

10

Arkady Cruz bounced through the jungle in the passenger seat of the bastardized Suzuki Jeep. Originally an old Jimmy 4X4, it now had solid axles, long travel coil springs, and the wheels were jacked up more than eighteen inches above normal. There was a roll cage but no roof and the bumpers were made out of spare tires front and back. A .50-caliber machine gun poked up above the roll cage. As well as the uniformed driver, there was another man on the machine gun and a third crouched in the back armed with an FX-05 Xiuhcoatl short-barreled assault rifle, the same general infantry weapon used by the Mexican army. Guzman might be a homicidal megalomaniac, but he was a well-equipped one.

The jungle buggy moved quickly down the narrow pathway through the surprisingly light foliage. The ground was dry, open to the sun with large stands of narrow trees and twisting vines. The trails were well defined and old, most of them in use by animals and man for hundreds of generations.

An hour's journey brought them to a clearing at the foot of an old Mayan temple, crumbled and almost nonexistent. The clearing had been laid out like an old Roman fort with the small ruins in the center. An earthen berm had been thrown up and topped with a bamboo palisade. Within the rectangular space were three dozen huts laid out in neat rows and a central building directly in front of the ruins. The huts were all raised on posts, the roofs made from flattened fifty-gallon drums. *In a heavy rain the roofs would sound like a steel band playing*, thought Arkady.

There were uniformed men everywhere: marching in the narrow streets, practicing drill, standing guard on the bamboo palisade, manning the machine guns in the towers at the four corners of the compound, and doing various bits of domestic camp business like cleaning latrines, preparing food, and even hanging laundry.

The camp was a small town, all men, all in uniform, and all with hard expressions on their long-nosed Mayan faces. They had the serious look of Castro's old comrades from the early days of the revolution. That's what Guzman was promising, a return of Mayan rule to Mayan land. Drugs and money under the guise of revolution. An old story.

At the far end of the compound was an old-fashioned metal Quonset hut, roughly camouflaged with netting threaded with bits of foliage. There was a large generator humming beside it, and the Cuban submariner could see several large air-conditioning units poking through the curving walls. The factory.

Somewhere in the nearby hill territory farther inland there would be camouflaged plantations of opium poppies, and closer in to the camp there would be an airfield. Guzman produced very little opium base on his own, preferring to import it from elsewhere, mostly Venezuela and Guatemala. The opium base would be refined into morphine in his little factory, then sent to Cuba with Arkady for final processing into heroin.

The stripped-down Jeep pulled up in front of the large building under the shadow of the temple ruins. Guzman was waiting for him on the shaded porch of the headquarters building. He was not your average Mexican drug lord. He looked more like a middle-aged accountant.

His black hair was thinning, his eyes were distorted behind large, square-framed glasses, and he was at least fifty pounds overweight, a definite beer belly slopping over the waistband of his uniform trousers. The uniform itself had no sign of rank or status. There was an ink stain on the breast pocket of his shirt and more stains on his fingers, which were short and stubby, like a butcher's. Guzman smiled as Arkady climbed out of the jungle buggy.

"Capitaine Cruz, good morning to you!" The man's voice was sharp, almost feminine.

"And to you, Jefe," answered Cruz.

"A good trip?"

"I prefer the sea."

"Good!" Guzman answered. He gave a braying laugh, once again almost girlish. "You will rule the waves, I shall rule the jungle." His plump lips parted, showing off a very expensive set of capped teeth. "A good accommodation, don't you agree?"

"Whatever you say, Jefe."

"Come in to my parlor, have a drink," said Guzman. He turned without waiting for an answer and marched back into the headquarters building. Cruz went up the steps. The driver of the jungle buggy lit a cigarette and waited.

The interior of the headquarters was sparse. The single room was large, the floor covered with a thin straw mat. There was a cot and a chest of drawers at the far end of the room, a desk, several chairs, and a wall map of the Yucatán Peninsula behind the desk. There was also a bar made from a small washstand and a huge Victorian plush velvet couch with three matching chairs arranged in a little social grouping around a cold woodstove. The velvet on the couch and chairs was a worn whore-house red.

A thin, pale-faced man in a white jacket appeared out of nowhere carrying a tray with one hand. His other hand and arm were missing, the sleeve of his jacket pinned to his shoulder. There were two cups of coffee on the tray, a silver sugar bowl, and a cream jug, also silver. The cups were Meissen Blue Onion porcelain. The one-armed man placed the tray on the top surface of the woodstove, then disappeared.

Guzman came back from where he'd been standing at the washstand bar carrying a squat, dark bottle of Azteca de Oro brandy. He filled his coffee cup to the rim, then gestured with the bottle toward Arkady, who shook his head, declining the offer.

"Milk, sugar?"

"Black."

"Of course. You are Cuban." The drug lord tucked the brandy under his arm, picked up both cups without their saucers, and handed the nonalcoholic cup to Arkady. He sat down on the couch. Arkady settled into one of the velvet chairs and waited. Guzman swallowed half his adulterated coffee in a single gulp, then filled it again from the brandy bottle.

"What do you think?"

"Of the coffee?" Arkady took a sip. "It's quite good." In fact it was bitter, only half roasted and probably local.

"It's shit." Guzman grinned, showing off his American teeth again. "That's why I put the brandy in it."

Arkady smiled. Anyone who drank that much brandy before noon wasn't using it to disguise the taste of bad coffee.

"I see," said the Cuban, keeping his tone neutral.

"No, you don't. You don't see anything. That's why you're here."

Arkady shrugged and said nothing.

"I meant what do you think of my little camp?"

"Very efficient."

"Roman." Guzman nodded. "Identical to the kind that Caesar designed for his legions."

Arkady knew that Julius Caesar had never designed a military camp in his life and used a design that had been invented several hundred years before, but he said nothing. Silence in the presence of a madman seemed like the most prudent course.

"You're wondering why I had you brought to the camp."

"We generally meet on the beach."

"You were surprised?"

"Intrigued."

"Why do you think I asked you here?"

"I have no idea, Jefe."

"Perhaps I want to kill you. Perhaps I have decided to make an example of you to your masters. Perhaps I think I have been cheated out of what I feel is rightfully mine. Perhaps, as the Americans are so fond of telling the press, I am a raving madman who wants nothing more than to take a machete and take off your head or rip out your heart on a stone altar."

"A great many 'perhaps,' Jefe."

Guzman laughed. "Aren't you the cool one, Capitaine Cruz."

"Just practical." Cruz shrugged. "If you did any of those things my submarine would go back to Cuba, never to return. Your pipeline to the United States and your source of high-quality heroin refining would vanish overnight. As would the revenue you need to finance your revolution." The madman was insane but he wasn't stupid.

"Quite correct, Capitaine."

"So there has to be another reason."

"There is." Guzman showed off his teeth again.

Arkady let a small simmering hint of his exasperation reveal itself. "I have a large submarine waiting for me offshore, Señor Guzman. My men are breathing canned air and keeping silent to avoid detection by the sonobuoys the Americans scatter around the coastal waters of the Yucatán to stop men like you from plying your trade."

Guzman ignored the not so thickly veiled insult. The smile remained. He leaned forward on the couch and crooked a meaty forefinger at Arkady. The Cuban leaned forward.

"I have something to show you," the drug lord whispered. "Come with me."

Guzman put his empty cup on the floor and stood, still carrying the brandy bottle. He grabbed a battered and stained red beret from the desk, jammed it on his head at a rakish angle, and went outside again. Arkady followed him. They went down the steps to the jungle buggy, and Guzman dismissed the driver with a flick of his hand and a grunted order.

"I'll drive," he said to the Cuban. Cruz climbed into the passenger seat once again. Guzman fired up the Jeep, jammed it into four-wheel drive and roared off through the camp, leaving it through the far gate. He slewed onto an almost invisible track and battered his way into the jungle.

"In 1962 I was a young boy living in a village near here called Nohcacab. It was a small place of no account in the middle of the jungle. Once, in the nineteenth century, some Dutch and German settlers tried to farm the land. Most were slaughtered in the Caste Wars in 1848, but there was some small amount of intermarrying of which my family was the result."

"You seem to know a lot about it."

"It is my heritage, my legacy. I did a great deal of research, Capitaine." He took a sharp turn onto an even narrower track, underbrush pressing in on either side of the Jeep as it bullied its way through the jungle.

"In 1962, you were a young boy," Cruz reminded the man.

"In 1962, on Christmas Eve there was a terrible storm in the skies above our village. The elders thought it was a bad omen. We were Catholics, but in the jungle the old ways survived under the surface. Somehow Chac, the god of thunder and lightning, had been offended. To confirm this there was a sudden blaze directly above the village, clearly visible. An explosion. I saw it myself. I remember it clearly. We all thought it was the end of the world."

"What happened?"

"The burning man," said Guzman. "A figure hurtling from the sky wreathed in fire, like a comet coming to earth. He struck one of the houses, igniting the roof thatch even though it was soaked with rain. For a moment the people of the village did nothing, but eventually an elder stepped forward and went into the hut where the burning man had struck. I remember that everyone was very frightened but no one looked away."

A burning man, thought Arkady; *he really is out of his mind*. The Jeep came out into a clearing in the jungle. It seemed like it was a natural formation, a sloping meadow leading down to a narrow crease in the forest floor. Just at the head of the crease was a mound, fifty or sixty feet high, and a long cigar-shaped uplift of foliage behind it like a vine- and earth-covered trail left by some enormous digging animal. After Guzman's little speech Arkady had imagined they were going to the remains of Guzman's old village, but there was no sign of that here. The mound was regularly shaped, four-sided, and impossibly abrupt: the classic pattern of a small buried Aztec pyramid, obviously untouched by the curious hands of modern archaeologists. The mound was a blaze of golden blossoms and large leathery leaves, almost obscenely glossy, that grew on long trailing vines, thousands of them twisted together to form a woody, impenetrable barrier.

"They are called yellow allamanda," said Guzman as he pulled the Jeep to a stop. "*Allamanda cathartica* is the Latin name."

"*Cathartica*, as in laxative?" Arkady guessed.

"The whole plant is poisonous. You'd swell up like a balloon if you were stupid enough to eat it. Then you'd foul your trousers for a day or two. Not fatal, though."

"You didn't bring me out here to look at flowers," said Arkady.

"No," said Guzman. He walked down through the grasses of the sloping meadow to the cigar-shaped hump of risen earth at the base of the pyramid. He extended a hand dramatically. "I brought you here to show you this."

Arkady joined him. He looked.

"It looks like the grave of the giant in the beanstalk story," said the Cuban skeptically.

"Funny, yes, but partially true." Guzman stepped forward and pulled back a section of camouflage netting. Beneath the netting was a jagged opening. The edges of the opening were shining silver. Aluminum. Guzman eased himself through the opening and disappeared. Hesitantly, Arkady followed. Guzman switched on a hissing Coleman gas lantern. It was like being inside the belly of a metal monster, steel ribs curving left and right.

Wires, heavy with mold, hung everywhere. Guzman crept forward, his back hunched in the cramped space.

"There," he said, lifting the lamp so Arkady could see clearly.

The object was almost fifteen feet long, tubular with stubby wings, held in some kind of heavy metal cradle at either end.

"What is this?" asked Arkady, his voice low, fearing that he already knew the answer.

"This is the midsection of the fuselage of a B-47 bomber, the one they used to call the Stratofortress. The item in front of you is one of Saddam Hussein's hidden weapons of mass destruction. It was here all the time! Imagine that! Your president Bush was right all along!" Guzman bellowed with laughter, the sound tinny in the enclosed space.

"It's a bomb," Arkady murmured.

"It is more than that, Capitaine Cruz," said Guzman. "It is a lever big enough to move the world. It is the future of your country, if you wish it." The lunatic paused for effect. "It is a Mark 28 free-fall B28RN model 5, 1.45-megaton thermonuclear device. A hydrogen bomb."

"*Pizda na palochke*," whispered Arkady. "We're in trouble now."

11

The *Hispaniola* made the run from Nassau to Bimini in an easygoing fifteen hours, arriving just before dawn and anchoring off North Rock in twenty-three feet of crystal-clear water. Miami wasn't even a smudge on the horizon fifty miles to the east. The day was a jewel. There wasn't much traffic except for a few overeager tourists and their guides in flat-boats looking for bonefish in the shallows, and no one seemed to pay them much attention.

On the other hand, Finn and Billy knew that word of their arrival would get around the little community on the fishhook-shaped island within hours. Bimini, like any small town, lived and breathed gossip.

"It's a bit like a dream," said Billy, leaning on the main deck rail. "All this larking about, looking for ancient treasure maps and haring after Aztec gold. Not the sort of thing my father would have called honest labor."

"What did your father do?"

"He was a member of parliament."

"That's honest labor?" Finn scoffed. "That's like saying politicians never lie."

"Still…"

"My father and my mother both spent their lives digging up the past. They made history live again."

"Most people think history is a waste of time."

"Then most people aren't thinking straight. Everything we are now is the result of an accumulation of things we've done in the past. By examining what we did we can figure out what to do or not to do in the future. By looking for trade routes to the East the Spaniards discovered the West. Without them and the technology that allowed people like Cortéz to get here, there wouldn't be a Miami over there."

"That might be a blessing."

"If we didn't study the Aztecs and why they suddenly vanished, we wouldn't understand modern ecology—they died out because of overfarming and famine, not wars. It's all tied together, and it certainly is honest labor."

"Is that what this is, or is it just a bunch of greedy sods looking for adventure?"

"You're certainly in a mood," said Finn, glancing at her gloomy friend.

"I guess I'm having one of those 'what is the meaning of life?' moments," murmured Billy.

It was Finn's turn to sigh.

"If we'd never met what would you be doing right now?" she asked.

"Trying to sell some piece of the family estate so that I could buy a new bilge pump for my boat." He snorted. "The one the buggers blew up almost under our feet in Amsterdam a while ago."

"And that's honest labor? Is that the meaning of life? Who says you can't have some fun along the way? Who says the world doesn't need a little more adventure these days?"

"I suppose it's my Calvinist background," said Billy. "Nose to the grindstone and all that." He shrugged his shoulders. "I suppose I thought I was going to mess around in boats until I noticed the first gray hair, then get down to serious business."

"Doing what?"

"Something meaningful, I suppose."

"You've got a postgraduate degree in Spanish literature from Oxford and you did your dissertation on the thrillers of John D. Macdonald. How meaningful is that... Dr. Pilgrim?"

"I suppose I'd have been a teacher."

"Teaching other people how to be teachers," said Finn. "I was brought up to believe it was the journey, not the destination."

"I suppose you think I'm being silly." Billy sighed.

"No," said Finn, "I *know* you're being silly."

Eli Santoro stepped out of the deckhouse a few feet away.

"We've got something on the side scan coming in," said the one-eyed man. "Right where you said it would be."

Finn and Billy followed him back into the long low-ceilinged cabin. It was crammed with every possible kind of electronic device from monitor screens for the robot television cameras to GPS displays, weather radar, the magnetic anomaly "fish-finder" echo-sounding array and the side-scanning sonar.

Guido Derlagen sat in front of the color screen of the side-scan unit and tweaked the dials on the image. It looked like the print of an old hobnail boot, slightly wider in the center and narrower at one end.

"Three masts. High at bow and stern. A *nau*, a carrack. About eighty or ninety feet long," said the Dutchman. "Thirty feet down on a sandy bottom."

"Aye," commented Run-Run McSeveney from where he was perched on a counter by the door and sipping from an old enamel cup. "Or it could verra well be naught but a blodgy bit o' coral where it oughtn't ought to be." His face screwed up. "Why hasn't anyone seen it before if it was that easy?"

"It's right there on the charts," said Eli Santoro. "Shifting sandbars. It's an undersea sand river. There's been a lot of hurricane activity the last few years. Al Gore weather. It was probably buried before."

"And it still could be a blodgy bit o' coral."

"You really are a sour old bugger, aren't you?" Billy laughed.

"I'm a Scot. We're sour by nature. It's the bluidy winters in Auld Reekie," answered the skinny little man with a gold-capped grimace. "But I'm philosophical about it, which is the Chinee in me."

"You're all crazy," said Finn. "Now, who wants to dive?"

She moved through the water smoothly, arms at her sides. The big Dacor fins pumped in a smooth slow rhythm, propelling her through the warm clear depths, the tanks on her back a comforting weight as she swam down the wreck site. The position on the side scan had been five hundred yards or so from where the *Hispaniola* was anchored, and they were using the twelve-foot Zodiac 420 they kept as a tender on the chart room roof for a dive boat.

Being in the water was a relief after the long jet trip from Heathrow and the journey across England and half of Europe that had gone before. Sometimes it seemed to Finn that she'd spent half her young life in some kind of academic surroundings, like universities and archives like the one in Spain, and while she enjoyed the challenge of research, sometimes she craved the adventure of being on-site. Her father and mother had been the same way: when they were annotating finds back in Columbus they were yearning for the jungle, and vice versa. Archaeology was like that: half the time spent looking and the other half spent studying what you found.

She smiled to herself around the silicone mouthpiece she had gripped between her teeth. Study was over, the hunt had begun, and the first scent of the quarry was right below her in the glowing sand at the bottom of the Florida Straits.

Briney Hanson stood at the rail on the flying bridge of the *Hispaniola* smoking one of his clove cigarettes and occasionally peering through the pair of binoculars that hung around his neck, a vintage Zeiss instrument he had owned for years and his last link with the old *Batavia Queen*. He smiled, squinting in the sunlight as he looked out to the Zodiac bobbing in the small waves a quarter of a mile away.

He'd come a long way from the little Danish coastal town of Thorsminde. He was the son of a herring fisherman by way of the South China Sea, and had spent his adult life piloting old rust buckets like the *Queen* on their tramping routes from one fly-blown island port to another, going nowhere slowly and calling no place home.

And now here he was, riding the tide off Miami Beach and master of a ship outfitted with everything except a hot tub. His home port was an island paradise, and except for occasional groups of Colombians in superfast cigarette boats trying to outdo *Miami Vice*, it was all relatively peaceful. It was almost enough to make him feel guilty.

He took a last puff on the Djarum cigarette and snuffed it out in the makeshift ashtray he'd duct-taped to the bridge rail—a coffee tin filled with beach sand, another holdover from his days on the *Batavia Queen*. Finn was forever giving him lectures about his nicotine habit, but he was a stubborn advocate. One of these days he was going to find himself being the last smoker on the planet.

He lifted the glasses again and looked out at the Zodiac. Finn, his lordship, and the Dutchman were all in the water; the little inflatable was empty. It was safe enough though; there were two buoys bobbing in the water on either side of the rubber boat, each flying the distinctive red and white "Diver Down" pennant.

He moved the glasses over the water. It was uniformly shallow, sunlight reflecting easily back from the sandy bottom, the terrain mottled with darker areas showing a few deepwater trenches and one or two of the circular formations called blue holes, which were relatively common in the Bahamas Banks.

The holes had been formed before the last ice age when the entire Bahamas Plateau had been above sea level, the limestone formations creating sinkholes as the rock weathered naturally over time. Because of the poor circulation of water in most Blue Holes, the water was anoxic—sometimes completely devoid of any free oxygen at all and utterly devoid of any marine life. According to the side-scanning sonar, the wreck Finn and the others were investigating was only a few yards from one of the formations. A little bit to one side and the ship would have slid into the hole and vanished, never to be found again.

Hanson refocused the binoculars and looked a little farther out. According to the information Finn and Lord Billy had been given by the antiquarian book dealer in Paris, the *San Anton* had gone down on a line between the shoals on the upper end of North Bimini Island, now called the Bluff, and a limestone formation three hundred yards out and only visible at low tide called North Rock.

According to the detailed charts, the water varied from twenty to thirty feet over most of the area, sloping upward to shoals at the island end and dropping off abruptly into water hundreds of feet deep on the Florida Strait side.

The captain's log of the *San Anton* said the ship had been blown into the shallows during the hurricane, foundered on the shoals, and sank just offshore. Also according to the log, the *San Anton* had been carrying a small cargo of spices, mostly pepper, and had not been worth attempting any kind of salvage operation. On the other hand, as Lord Billy had pointed out, if the ship had no cargo worth salvaging, why had the captain made such a detailed report of exactly where she had gone down?

Hanson put down the glasses and lit another cigarette. The whole thing was beyond him; he was still getting used to a regular paycheck and a tropical home base, not to mention the joys of not having to deal with cargoes of banana chips, raw rubber, and once, a nightmarish load of liquid guano. He lifted the glasses and made another careful sweep of the surface.

There was nothing to see except the sun glinting brilliantly off the small turquoise waves stretching to the horizon. He closed his eyes and let his senses hold the moment. He smiled to himself, feeling the warmth of the tropical sun on his tanned, handsome face. This was what he needed, clear sailing and nothing looming on the horizon.

Finn floated above the wreck while Billy and Guido did a photographic survey, Billy using one of the big Nikonos digital cameras and Guido holding a two-meter graded survey stick for scale. Before giving up his job as a corporate lawyer in Amsterdam, the muscular Dutchman's idea of adventure had been thrice-weekly visits to the gym. He hadn't even known how to swim.

Like everything else he did, however, Guido never took on a challenge by halves. Eighteen months later and he swam better than Finn and was an expert diver to boot. On top of that he was reading anthropology and archaeology texts by the bushel, and was getting Briney Hanson to teach him celestial navigation.

Finn stared down at the shape in the sand beneath her. There was no doubt in her mind that it was the *San Anton*, lost here in July of 1521 under the command of Captain Gonzalo Rodriguez, the man who had kept the log shown to them by Pierre Jumaire in Paris. The ship was no more than eighty feet long and would have fit easily in the space between home plate and first base on a regulation baseball diamond.

The *nau*, which simply meant "ship" in Spanish, were the last of a long line of watercraft that went back centuries, the front and rear of the vessel literally built as forts from which archers and spearmen could engage other ships. In the case of the *San Anton*, the "fort" that made up the fo'c'sle, or forecastle, of the ship was eight or ten feet above the sand. The rear quarterdeck was not quite as clearly defined.

The main deck of the wreck was completely covered by sand and the only evidence that there was even a center portion was the stump of the mainmast poking up darkly from the tongue of sand, which lay like an unmoving river that pointed toward the lip of the blue hole less than a hundred feet away. It was clear that the ship was leaning steeply to one side, and Finn knew they'd had the luck of the Irish on their side. Another hurricane and the ship might well have been pulled inexorably into the depths of the vertical limestone cave and probably torn to pieces in the process.

Finn let herself drift down toward the ship as Billy finished up the photo survey. She swam the length of the wreck, looking for some way into the hull. If Jumaire was right, Captain Rodriguez knew that he was carrying something extremely valuable back to his masters in Spain, and he'd most probably kept it close.

If the copy of the Cortéz Codex really was on board, it would probably still be in the captain's cabin, located under the quarterdeck. At first glance Finn couldn't see an opening, which meant they'd have to break out the big vacuum pumps and hoses to flush the excess sand out of the way. If they went deep enough they'd probably find a hole in the bottom of the ship created when she'd foundered on the nearby shoals during the hurricane, but coming in from the bottom in a shifting sandbar would be dangerous. Finding a way in from the deck would be far safer.

She paused, turning herself slightly in the water. She heard something in the distance, a faint vibration like a faraway drumbeat of thunder. A boat. She looked up automatically, searching for and finding the shadow of the Zodiac on the surface and the thin anchor line that led down toward the wreck. They'd been careful to put out Diver Down buoys, so she wasn't really worried. It was probably just a local coming out to take a look at the *Hispaniola*. She turned back to her examination of the wreck.

Hanson heard the boat before he saw it; a heavy sound of big diesels somewhere to the east and the churning slap and heavy whisper of a bow wave. Even without seeing it, Briney knew the boat was large; there was no outboard whine or harsh slapping sound of a planing fiberglass hull smacking down into the water. A workboat of some kind. He turned the glasses toward the channel between North Rock and the Bluff, waiting apprehensively. With the buoys out and the Zodiac clearly visible, he wasn't too worried, but any kind of large vessel in the area was potentially a problem, and accidents happened, even in perfect weather like this.

Suddenly the ship appeared. She was a shallow-draft trawler, half the size of the *Hispaniola* and old. The hull had once been painted smuggler's gray but was now streaked with rust the color of old dried blood. She had a single funnel pumping black smoke in a stream behind her as her bow broke heavily in the pale water, throwing up an arc of foam. Both of her swinging booms were out and she was going full speed, her course clearly taking her directly toward the Zodiac.

Run-Run McSeveney had felt the vibration of her passage down in the engine room and had burst out onto the deck below Hanson's position. Both men saw the danger immediately.

"The bluidy bampot! What in the name of God is he thinkin'?"

The trawler was a long liner, running two sets of lines from the masts. Each line was connected to a pair of steadying otter boards beneath the water to keep her depth constant. The lines were separated into sublines, or "snoods," each of the snoods carrying hundreds of baited hooks. Running two lines like this one, the trawler could be dragging literally thousands of deadly hooks through the water at an unknown depth. A diver snagged on the lines could be torn to shreds in seconds or just as easily dragged for miles and drowned.

Hanson hurled himself down the companionway ladder to the bridge and lunged toward the large red button on the main console beside the throttles. He hammered his palm down on the button again and again, sounding the big Kahlenberg S2 air horns, sending out a deep-throated wail that could have come from a speeding freight train bearing down on the fishing boat.

"Why doesn't the pikslikker change course?!" Hanson bellowed, swearing in Danish.

Run-Run appeared on the bridge, chest heaving.

"The geggie hoer-slet isn't going to stop!"

"Weigh anchor!" Hanson yelled. Run-Run jumped to the console and hit the main winch controls and the anchor chain began to wind up forward with agonizing slowness. Hanson knew they didn't have much time. As soon as he felt the slight shudder of the big Danforth fluke anchor pulling from the sandy bottom, Hanson pulled the twin throttles down, taking the powerful diesels from idle to all ahead full in a split second. As soon as the big converted tug gained a fractional headway Hanson spun the big wheel hard to port in a desperate attempt to cut the trawler off. It was going to be very close.

Finn was swimming down the exposed side of the wreck when she caught a hint of movement at the edge of her vision and heard a heavy clanking sound. Looking up, she spotted Guido banging the back of his air tank with the handle of his dive knife and waving his right arm up and down: the signal for danger. Spotting her looking, he turned and pointed to the east. Finn stared.

There was a huge shadow above them coming in at a high rate of speed, and in the shadow's wake glinted a thousand points of light deep in the water. It took her a few seconds to realize what she was seeing. The shadow was a trawler heading toward the Zodiac and the twinkling flares in the water were bright steel fishhooks catching the light of the morning sun. The hooks were spread out in a line at least five hundred feet across and coming closer by the second.

Billy appeared on her left, the camera hooked to his dive belt. He grabbed her by the arm and pushed her down toward the sandy bottom. She nodded and kept pace, finding a shallow niche under the curving side of the wreck. An instant later Guido joined them.

The thundering of the trawler's engine was pounding in Finn's ears now. Guido signaled, three fingers of one hand hooked into a claw. He pointed up and Finn nodded, realizing what he was trying to tell her and Billy:

if there were enough hooks in the array of connecting lines trailing behind the trawler, they could easily have enough power to hook the wreck and pull it over on them, crushing the three divers underneath the hull. There was no chance of reaching the surface without being impaled. There was no place to go unless they tried to make it to the lip of the blue hole a hundred feet away.

Then Billy spotted another avenue of escape. He squeezed Finn's shoulder and turned her around, pointing. At her feet she could see a faint dark and jagged line where the hull met the sand. Twisting, all three divers turned themselves downward in the water and began to dig frantically at the sand with their bare hands. The pounding of the trawler's engines was even louder now. On the bottom the ragged hole in the hull of the *San Anton* grew fractionally larger and Finn saw what it was: the remains of an old gun port in the stern section, now half buried. A way into the ship.

Running at a full twelve knots, the anchor winch howling and the diesels thundering, the *Hispaniola* headed directly at the trawler. The tug was almost twice the size of the trawler, and even a glancing blow from the *Hispaniola* would capsize her. The trawler never faltered; a few moments later the Zodiac and the Diver Down buoys disappeared under her foaming bow. Hanson altered course fractionally. It was too late to ram the trawler but there was still a chance.

"There's na name on the blaigeard's bow!" Run-Run yelled over the sound of the engines. "The fannybawz is a gedgie pirate!"

Hanson risked a quick look. The engineer was right; the trawler's name, along with her license registration, had been obscured with heavy grease or paint. If she escaped out into the Florida Straits she'd disappear in a few short hours into fleets of fishing boats that plied these waters.

"How close are we?"

"Hundred yards," answered Run-Run with an experienced eye. "We might take her in the stern but it'll be a near thing with the anchor dragging at us like it is."

"How much chain is still out?"

Run-Run looked down at the winch gauge. "Twenty feet," he called out.

"That should do it," Hanson said with a tight, angry grimace on his face. "Hang on, old man!"

Hispaniola seemed to rise to the occasion, her bow leaping upward as the anchor chain shortened and the drag on her forward momentum changed. The big tug shouldered through the water, the sea churning up a broad wake behind her as she raced forward, coming within a few short yards of clipping the stern of the other vessel.

"Nowt on transom neither, the cladaire bastrid!" Run-Run yelled out as they passed. Out of the corner of his eye Hanson saw that the engineer was right; the name and home port on the stern had been obscured as well.

There was a staggering lurch as the Danforth anchor and its heavy chain connected with the twin cables stretched out from the trawler's outriggers, tearing through them and snapping the heavy mahogany booms into broken, splintered stumps on the smaller ship's deck.

The cables tore away, wrapping around the anchor chain as the *Hispaniola* dragged the long lines and the multiple hook snoods away from the dive sight. Still moving at full speed, the fouled anchor came banging up out of the water to rest against the hull, trailing the cables like dragging lengths of seaweed.

Hanson put the *Hispaniola* into a broad turn, taking them around the jagged mass of North Rock, then slowed and finally stopped. Now on the starboard side, the trawler was pounding off into the distance. There was no question of going after her; the propeller would eventually foul in the dragging lines, and it was more important to see to the safety of Finn and the others. Hanson lifted the binoculars, aiming them at the position where the Zodiac had been. There were only a few pieces of floating wreckage to mark the spot.

"Can ye see anything?" McSeveney said anxiously.

"No, nothing," Hanson answered. "Not a damn thing."

12

Cardinal Enrico Michelangelo Rossi, assistant secretary of state for the Vatican, strolled down the central pathway in the immense Cortile del Belvedere, the Courtyard of the Belvedere, heading toward the huge bronze statue of a pinecone, the famous *Pigna*, which had once been a centerpiece of one of the court-yard's many fountains. The fountains were long gone, the Belvedere now transformed into a simple lawn with one of Arnaldo Pomodoro's gold-tinted, brightly reflective *Sfera con Sfera*, or *Sphere within a Sphere*, as though trying to prove the "New" Church's humble simplicity.

The old man smiled at the thought. He was walking through the most valuable piece of property in Rome, surrounded by buildings of immense architectural significance and filled with priceless works of art, all paid for by the sweat of the brows of millions of the impoverished. All of it ws tax-free and based on a promise of immortality and paradise that had to be one of the world's great fairy tales and insurance sales pitches combined.

Cardinal Rossi was, above all things, a practical man; faith in the Church was the bedrock of his life. Faith in a benevolent god or any god at all was something else again. He saw no conflict in this. Thomas the Apostle had doubted the Resurrection until he felt Christ's wounds for himself. Rossi would believe in Heaven and Hell when he arrived at one destination or the other. Until then he would reserve judgment, knowing that the work he did on this earth was work to further the safety of the Church and not incidentally his own ambitions within it.

The man walking beside him was dressed in the plain robes of a parish priest, a costume he had no right to wear but one that gave him easy access to the Vatican and anywhere else he chose to go in Rome; there was nothing that sank into the background of the city's awareness more than the sight of a Catholic priest. He had dark hair and wore thick glasses. His most recent service to the cardinal had been the execution of a book dealer in Paris.

The cardinal spoke softly.

"It went well?"

"There were no problems."

"The book?"

"He'd already given it to them."

"How do you know?"

"I saw them go into the store earlier. They came out with a small package wrapped in paper. I assumed it was not a coincidence."

"Then why kill him?"

"You told me to."

"To prevent them discovering the location of the ship."

"I was too late to do the one so I did the other."

"You're sure it was them?"

"The same people I followed in Seville, yes. The pretty one with the red hair and the English lord."

"Their continued existence complicates things. There is a long skein connecting the parties to this. It would be a disaster to *Cavallo Nero* if the skein led back to me. It would be a disaster for the entire Church. We cannot be tied to events in any way."

"I'm always at your disposal, Eminence," said the man in the thick glasses.

The cardinal frowned at the thought that the man might be making a play on words at his expense.

"Like a faithful hound, is that it?"

"We are all the Dogs of God," the false priest answered.

"That is hardly the point," replied the cardinal. He stopped below the raised stone platform holding the aging greenish bronze pinecone and stared up at it, trying to remember what the religious significance of it was and failing. So many saints, sinners, and signs in the heavens. It was hard to keep track of this place's long and convoluted mythology. It seemed to change with each passing year. Once St. Christopher had been revered, and now he was just a million small medals hooked over a million truck drivers' rearview mirrors. Even St. Valentine had been debunked, apparently nothing more than an invention of Geoffrey Chaucer and his Parliament of Fools.

"I wonder who the patron saint of murderers is?" Cardinal Rossi asked himself.

"Saint Guntramnus," said the man standing beside him. "He called a doctor to cure his dying wife, and when the doctor couldn't help her, Guntramnus slit his throat with a razor."

"Trust you to know," murmured the cardinal. He turned and began to walk back down the path to Pomodoro's shining statue of a shattered sphere. "Contact Guzman. Tell him about these treasure seekers. They must be dealt with discreetly and with dispatch. No errors this time."

"As you wish." The man nodded.

"*Bene*," said the cardinal. "Now leave me." He gave the assassin a two-fingered blessing. A group of tourist nuns in old-fashioned wimpled habits fluttered by like a flock of pink-faced black-and-white seagulls, inevitably plump. He gave them another blessing and each one paused, bowed, and made a brief sign of the cross, muttering a quick "God have mercy" as they passed by. He turned back to the man with the thick glasses, but he was already gone.

"Go with God," he said, not meaning a word of it.

Cat Cay is a private island just south of Bimini that advertises itself as one of Henry Morgan's treasure havens, a key base for Confederate blockade runners, a PT boat base during the Second World War, and the place where the Duke of Windsor introduced "Kiltie" fringed Oxford golf shoes and Argyle socks to the unsuspecting public.

In actual fact, it is a small, nondescript island in the Bimini chain closest to Miami, and was a well-known rendezvous and storage depot for rumrunners during Prohibition as well as a convenient spot for small- and big-time mobsters and politicians to congregate when they wanted to gamble and womanize. It also has great tuna fishing. Hemingway's last novel was set in the area, as the nouveau riche locals tell you endlessly. Its most recent development has come at the hands of the Rockwell family, the lowest bidders on most NASA contracts, including the Space Shuttle and its attendant problems over the years.

The island is shaped like a two-pronged fishhook with the fat part at the south end and the skinny part to the north. The fat part contains the nine-hole golf course once patronized by the Duke of Windsor and his patterned socks when he was governor general of the Bahamas during World War Two. The abdicated king played endless rounds of golf while his hawk-faced American wife popped over to Miami for a spot of unsupervised shopping.

Anyone with a well-aimed Big Bertha driver can hit a ball right across the island and into either the Atlantic or the Florida Straits, depending on which way they're facing. These days twenty-five thousand dollars gets you onto Cat Cay and a little more than half that amount keeps you there as long as the membership committee approves of the depth of your bank account and the length of your boat or your executive jet. In their time Al Capone, Meyer Lansky, Richard Nixon, Bebe Rebozo, and Spiro Agnew all loved to visit Cat Cay. The limestone speck's only other claim to fame is the invention of the tuna tower, an aluminum platform attached to a boat and used to spot fish.

James Noble stood at the tee on the seventh hole at Windsor Downs, put down his Maxfli Black Max ball, and angrily whacked the five-dollar-a-shot orb three hundred yards away over the trees and across the beach, and into the ocean.

"What the hell is the matter with you?" Noble asked his son, who was acting as his caddy. Although smoking on the course was strictly forbidden under club bylaws, the pharmaceutical magnate lit up a Cohiba Straight Pyramid cigar and sucked it into life on the end of his Dunhill lighter.

"I did exactly what you said," answered Harrison Noble.

"I told you to solve the problem, not announce it to the entire goddammed world. A fishing trawler? Jesus, Harrison!" The elder Noble put down a second ball and sent it after the first.

"I was trying to make it look like an accident."

"Did it work?"

"I didn't hang around to find out."

"So you might have done the job after all?"

"I don't know yet."

"And the trawler?"

"Haitian. One of the people the Mexican suggested."

"If they're still alive they'll know someone's onto them."

"There's no proof they even found anything."

"Find out."

"How am I supposed to do that?"

"Carefully," said the older man, putting down another ball. This time he tried to put it somewhere on the fairway between the tee and the green. It hooked to the left and wound up between the rough on the beach side and a yawning sand trap fifty feet away. He hated golf and was no good at it. He only played it because the casino didn't open until seven in the evening and his cardiologist had told him to exercise more.

He sucked on the cigar, hauling a huge cloud of sweet smoke into his lungs. He snorted out the smoke like a cartoon bull and stared at his son. It made him wonder about the human genome. Where James Noble was cold-blooded, Harrison Noble was hotheaded. Where the elder Noble was devious, the younger was foolishly transparent. The tree was strong, the branch was deadwood. His son was a blunt instrument. It was time to use him like one.

"Have them followed. Keep your distance. Don't do anything until I tell you to." He paused and took another heave on the cigar. "When the time comes, kill them. All of them. Dead this time."

"You told me all this before."

"This time listen to me."

Noble stomped off down the fairway, his son trailing behind him, humping the nine-thousand-dollar Louis Vuitton golf bag on his shoulder.

The lab on the *Hispaniola* had been converted from the original officers' wardroom on the oceangoing tug. It was located directly behind the lounge on the main deck, running almost all the way back to the stern and almost the full width of the vessel amidships. It was low-ceilinged, brightly lit, and had half a dozen rectangular portholes port and starboard. The outer perimeter was laid out with narrow counters for supplies and instrumentation, with the center of the room taken up by an eight-by-ten-foot translucent acrylic-topped examination table, diffusely lit from underneath. In Finn Ryan's mind it was the heart of everything they were doing.

She stood at the table wearing shorts and her favorite Thurman Café T-shirt. There was a large angry-colored bruise on her left leg and a long scrape on her right arm, but other than that she'd survived the trawler's attack relatively unscathed. Guido had fared a little worse, with half a dozen stitches on his cheek, which he thought might wind up giving him an attractively rakish dueling scar, and Billy walked with a painful limp from a stretched tendon. It had been a near miss for all three of them, and if Briney Hanson hadn't been able to sever the long line cable when he did, the wreck of the *San Anton* might have proved to be their watery grave. By the time Eli Santoro suited up and dived on the wreck, the five-hundred-year-old hulk was tipping dangerously toward the nearby blue hole, dragged there by a dozen or so snoods from the trawler's long line, which had fouled in the remains of the sunken ship's superstructure. As it was, the way in through the shattered hull had disappeared as the ship pitched over, and Eli had been forced to find another entrance into the wreck to rescue his friends, coming into the hull through the forecastle "sacre," a narrow port used to allow a cannon to fire directly forward. With the ship now dangerously unstable, there had been no time for a full-fledged inventory, but Finn had managed to retrieve one artifact from the half-destroyed captain's cabin before they surfaced once again. The artifact now sat on the examination table before them.

"What exactly are we looking at?" Briney Hanson asked, lighting up another of his perfumed clove cigarettes. Beside him Run-Run McSeveney wrinkled his nose at the smell, but even he knew better than to say anything.

"A lump, o' course," said the half-Chinese Scotsman.

"But a lump of what?" asked Guido. "It has the appearance of something very bad that sometimes floats to the surface of the canals in Amsterdam."

"I'm still not sure why you'd retrieve a thing like that in the first place," said Billy as they all stared at the object. "Not particularly attractive to my untrained eye." He shook his head. "I'm inclined to agree with Guido."

The object was a little more than a foot long, roughly tubular, and nine or ten inches in diameter. It had a dark, tarry surface and was slightly pinched at both ends. In a word, it was ugly.

"*Dàn juān*," said Run-Run.

"Don Juan?" Billy said. "What's he got to do with it?"

"*Dàn juān*," repeated the diminutive engineer. "Egg roll, ya sassenach gogan. I thought ya said ya went to Oxford Univairsity?"

"All right," said Billy, looking across at Finn on the other side of the table. "It's a fossilized bit of Chinese takeaway from five hundred years ago. It still doesn't explain why you hauled it back up on the *Hispaniola*."

"It's because it's so... useless," explained Finn. "You're right. It looks like..."

138

"It looks like a giant black taird," said Run-Run drily.

"Exactly," answered Finn with a smile. "So what's it doing in the captain's cabin? Why would he have such an ugly, unpleasant-looking thing in his possession?"

"What the dog did in the nighttime," Billy said and nodded.

"Ay?" said Run-Run.

"Sherlock Holmes," explained Billy.

"Ay?" Run-Run repeated.

"Another time," said Billy. "It's an Oxford thing."

Finn turned away from the table and checked the array of instruments laid out behind her. She slipped on a pair of latex surgical gloves from a dispenser, picked up a Stryker cast-cutting saw, and turned back to the table. She held down the long black object, and applied the blade of the little circular saw to the upper edge. She switched on the saw and trailed it down the length of the object applying almost no pressure.

"Phew!" Run-Run said, wrinkling his nose as a horrible stench filled the room.

"Burning rubber," muttered Briney Hanson.

"Gutta-percha," explained Finn, "or in this case, more probably chicle or gutta-balatá."

"Chicle, as in Chiclets?" Eli Santoro asked.

Finn nodded. "It was used to make chewing gum originally. Gutta-percha's a kind of rubber. They used it to insulate transatlantic cables. They still use it in dentistry.

Gutta-balatá is a Central American version, almost identical."

"Waterproofing," said Billy, suddenly understanding.

"That's it," said Finn. It took another five minutes with the saw to peel off the thick, slightly tarry layer of the gutta-balatá to reveal what lay beneath: a plain brown ceramic bottle with a wide neck covered in a second layer of sealing wax.

"A bottle?" Hanson asked.

"Probably for wine or rum," answered Finn.

"Quite a vintage, I should think," said Guido.

"I think the wine's all gone by now," said Billy.

Finn found a scalpel on the instrument table and spent another few minutes peeling and chipping away the wax seal. There was a lead-foil stopper beneath that, which she removed in turn. Finally the bottle was opened.

"Anything inside?" Billy asked.

Without answering Finn found a pair of rubber-tipped tongs and carefully inserted them into the broad opening at the top of the bottle. She pulled out a roll of odd-looking parchment, dry and perfect after half a millennia beneath the turquoise water of the Caribbean. Excited now, her fingers shaking slightly, she picked up a pair of tweezers and carefully unrolled the first inch of the roll. A row of brightly painted figures appeared: Aztec warriors.

Finn straightened and flipped back her long red hair. She was grinning from ear to ear.

"Gentlemen," she said, "I give you the Codex of Cortéz."

13

After returning to the submarine base in the ruined hull of the SS *Angela Harrison*, Arkady Cruz's next stop was the offices of Brigadier General Eduardo Delgado Rodriguez, head of the Dirección de Inteligencia, or DI, formerly known as Dirección General de Inteligencia, or DGI.

With the location of the offices on the corner of Linea and Avenue A in the Vedado section of Havana so well known it could be Googled by anyone with a computer, and under constant surveillance by various elements of the American intelligence community, including the satellites of the NSA, the CIA, the DIA, the DEA, the FBI, and Homeland Security, Cruz and his information were shuffled off to the North American directorate of DI, which had long since been moved out of Cuba altogether and was now headquartered in the embassy in Ottawa, Canada, a convenient three-hour plane ride to New York and easily accessible with direct flights from Havana by way of Toronto on Air Canada or Cubana Airlines.

The original embassy had been on Chapel Street in a quiet residential neighborhood of the city. The Embassy had been the target of so many American anti-Castro terrorist attacks from 1960 onward that it had been forced to move, finally becoming a purpose-built fortresslike structure in the suburban area known as Ottawa South.

After arriving in Toronto, Cruz rented a car using the identification of a Ukrainian businessman named Ignacy Gulka. From Pearson Airport he drove into the city, dropped the rental in the long-term lot at the Toronto Island Airport on the waterfront, and took a Porter Airline Bombardier Q400 turboprop for the one-hour jump to the nation's capital.

From Ottawa Airport he rented another car, this time as Xavier Martinez, a Bolivian coffee salesman, and drove to the center of the city. There he took a room at the Lord Elgin, a large old tourist hotel opposite the hexagonal bulk of the National Arts Centre.

Cruz then walked down Elgin Street to the florist on the corner of Somerset Street and purchased a red carnation for his lapel. Ten minutes later a black late-model Range Rover with smoked-glass windows pulled up at the light and Cruz stepped up into the passenger seat. A Yoruba black was behind the wheel wearing a dark suit and tie. He checked the flower in Cruz's lapel and then concentrated on his driving.

Fifteen minutes later they arrived at the embassy, a large, modern, two-and-a-half-story concrete slab with narrow, smoked-glass windows just like the ones on the

Range Rover. They drove directly down the ramp into the underground parking lot. Cruz spent a few minutes establishing his real identity at the security desk in the basement, then rode alone up the elevator to the top floor of the embassy. He walked down an anonymous, quietly carpeted hallway and stepped into the office of Brigadier General Rubén Martinez Puente.

Puente was a heavyset gray-haired man in his early sixties who could trace his involvement with Castro back to his teenage years during the first days of revolutionary power in Havana. He was now the head of Foreign Air Intelligence.

"Ah," said Puente from behind his large desk. "El Singular."

Cruz smiled. He'd heard the nickname before. The Only One. A comment on his abilities, perhaps, but more likely a wry and clearly antirevolutionary comment on the state of Cuba's navy and the size of its submarine fleet.

"Générale," said Cruz. There were no uniforms, but even so Cruz stood roughly at attention.

"Sit," said the general, gesturing toward a comfortable-looking armchair set at an angle to the desk. The office was cozy if a little rundown. A couch against one wall, out of style and upholstered in a worn-looking corduroy. A rug, Persian, but the kind of Persian the English had made in their cotton mills in the twenties, not from Iran or Afghanistan a century or more ago. The dark glass window looked out in perpetual artificial dusk over the backyards of neighborhood tract houses. The lights in the ceiling were buzzing fluorescents. The Supreme Leader's revolution was still alive but it was definitely ailing, just like El Supremo himself.

Cruz sat. The general spoke again.

"So, tell me about this thing you found in the jungle."

Cruz did so, describing exactly what he'd seen and the circumstances. It took fifteen minutes. He wondered if he'd traveled all this way just to make a quarter-of-an-hour report that no one wanted to believe.

"You're sure of the serial numbers?"

"Yes, sir. I wrote them down."

The general nodded. "They've been confirmed. They were manufactured in 1960 at the Pantex plant in Amarillo, Texas."

Cruz waited. The general stared at him for a moment, then picked up a red package of Populars from his desk and lit one with a very old-looking green Ronson. He didn't offer a cigarette to Cruz.

"We're concerned," said Puente.

"Yes, sir." Cruz had no idea who "we" referred to, nor did he think it politically wise to ask. In this day and age in Cuba the average man had no idea who belonged to what faction, or the degree of possible criminality that might be involved. From the moment he'd laid eyes on the bombs in the jungle, his primary objective had been to off-load the responsibility onto someone else's shoulders.

"The devices were lost on Nochebuena, Christmas Eve 1962."

"The missile crisis."

"At the time the Americans had a total of one hundred and seventy-eight Strategic Air Command flights in the air on any given day, each armed with at least one thermonuclear device. It was almost inevitable that there would be some kind of problem, either tactically or logistically. Given the times it is not surprising that the Americans did not make their so-called Broken Arrow incident public." The general drew heavily on the cigarette and then snorted smoke forcibly from his nostrils. "Presumably they thought the aircraft was lost on the outer leg of its flight, either in the Yucatán Channel or the gulf."

"Was there any search?"

"There were already a number of warships in the area, so yes, presumably. They couldn't very well tell the Mexican authorities that they'd lost a load of hydrogen bombs, could they?"

Cruz could tell that the man was thinking out loud now. "No, sir."

"The Americans are a very lazy lot. Out of sight, out of mind, I think the saying goes. Having the bombs fall on land was too much of a difficulty, so in their own minds it could not have happened, yes?"

"Yes, sir."

"But it did happen."

"Yes, sir."

"Which you have now brought to our attention." It almost sounded like an accusation.

"Yes, sir."

"So what are we going to do about it?"

In the earlier, black-and-white days of the revolution, they would simply have "disappeared" Cruz and the problem along with it, but practical considerations now made that difficult. And then there was Guzman, the wild card.

"I don't know, sir," answered Cruz. "What are we going to do about it?"

"This Guzman, the drug dealer, he assumes he can actually sell these things to us?"

"He thinks so."

"*Dios*," said Puente, shaking his head. He stubbed out his cigarette in a glass ashtray on his desk. "Is he mad?"

"Yes, sir," said Cruz. "Almost certainly. He thinks giving the weapons to us will make Cuba his ally. He wants to become dictator of Mexico. An Adolf Hitler of sorts."

"Or a Stalin?" Puente grinned.

"I don't think he cares either way, sir."

"Do you know how a hydrogen bomb works, Capitaine?"

"Vaguely, sir."

"It is like using a hand grenade to set off a fertilizer bomb. A nuclear explosion at one end sets off a plutonium bomb at the other. Fission creating fusion. A filthy thing. The weapons on the Strategic Air Command B-47's flying patterns around Cuba were all fused and operable. Do you know what this means?"

"That they're dangerous."

"Exactly. To try and transport two such devices through the jungle and on board your submarine would be an act of suicide."

"So?"

"So we do not want them. Also we do not want them in the hands of Señor Guzman."

"He prefers the title Generalissimo."

"I'm sure he does. At any rate, he cannot be allowed to have them and we do not want them. The question is, what do we do with them?"

"Tell the Americans where they are?"

"It had occurred to me, but it would be too complicated. The resolution would be out of our control."

"There is some other possibility?"

"I think so."

"Yes?"

"Yes. Our Chinese friends."

Since the demise of the Soviet Union, China had stepped in as Cuba's main military ally, especially in the field of intelligence gathering, notably at the Bejucal telecommunications center tapping into American military radio and satellite traffic. They had also heavily invested in developing Cuba's offshore oil potential.

"What can they do for us?" Cruz asked, wondering what his role in all this was.

"They can send us a nuclear team and some of their Special Forces personnel. There are some of them already in Cienfuegos. The nuclear team will detonate the bombs on-site."

"I beg your pardon?"

"The initiating package in the bombs is a form of high explosive. With the tritium core removed the explosive can be detonated safely. An unfused bomb was accidentally set off outside of Albuquerque, New Mexico. It made a crater twelve feet across and killed a cow."

"The generalissimo isn't going to like you neutralizing his prized possessions," commented Cruz.

Puente smiled. A gold molar flashed. The rest of his teeth were tobacco stained from too many Populars.

"The stupid *mamalon* can go *singarte un caballo*, for all I care. What do you think the Special Forces people are for?"

"He has his own people. A squad of body-guards."

"Buy them off."

"Their leader is Guzman's cousin."

"Buy him off as well."

"And if he won't be bought?"

"Anyone can be bought, Capitaine Cruz. Simply pay him more. If he doesn't take the money, give him his own head."

"What is my part in all of this?"

"Take the nuclear team and the Special Forces group to Guzman's camp. Put your generalissimo at his ease."

"How do I explain the Chinese gentlemen?"

"Tell Guzman they are prospective buyers. Make him believe it."

"If this works out as you have described, we will have a hole in our transportation network, Générale. It makes a great deal of money for the regime."

Puente leaned back in his chair and put the tips of his square, well-manicured fingers on the edge of the desk. He smiled again. The tooth gleamed.

"If there is one thing to know about drug lords, Capitaine, it is that there is a never-ending supply of them."

Max Kessler sat at his favorite table next to the pastry case at Leopold's Café enjoying his favorite breakfast of *Belgishe Zuckerwaffeln* with extra whipped cream on the side and his second *Verlangerter*, an Austrian version of a caffe latte. A little later he'd finish off his meal with an Esterhazy pastry and perhaps even a third coffee. He looked out through the bank of glass doors that led to the brick-paved courtyard and considered the problem at hand.

In point of fact it was less a problem than a situation, and perhaps, if everything he'd discovered was accurate, an opportunity for great gain, both financially and in terms of pure intelligence-gathering power. Kessler, who rarely talked to anyone at all unless it had to do with business, would never have described his profession in negative terms. In the unlikely event of being asked to do so, he would have portrayed himself as a fisherman casting a wide net and bringing in a varied catch from which he might create a single feast for his clients. In clinical and objective terms, however, it might have been better to depict himself as a gluttonous spider in the center of an enormous web, sinking his fangs into his victims' bodies, liquefying their internal organs and digesting the result.

In his case the web was a worldwide network of informants feeding him tidbits of apparently unrelated information, which he digested and then regurgitated in a single, meaningful purge, vague links solidified into a coherent mass. It was this ability to create a single picture from a jigsaw puzzle of tiny parts that was Max Kessler's true talent, as it had been his father's before him. He had no ulterior motive to cloud his judgment, so the pictures when they coalesced were perfectly clear and without bias. His only goal was the picture itself and the process of putting it together.

He was now in that part of the process where he was relatively sure he had all the pieces, with at least the outer edges of the picture being formed. Other pieces were also merging and only needed to be put together. He dipped his last piece of waffle in his little dish of whipped cream and popped it into his mouth, following the morsel with a sip of aromatic coffee. He gestured to the waiter. It was time for dessert.

The Esterhazy appeared, a multilayered torte with hazelnut filling. Max carved off a small teasing bite and let it melt in the center of his tongue, assembling his facts and staring blankly into space.

First, Harrison Noble, a mediocre treasure hunter whoring his way through the Caribbean, requests information about Angel Guzman, clearly at the direction of his pharmaceutical billionaire papa. Thus, a link between Guzman the *cocainista* and Father Noble.

Second, Fiona Ryan and Lord William Pilgrim, much more high-profile treasure seekers doing research in the Archives of the Indies in Seville, are observed being followed by a man known to be affiliated with Cardinal Enrico Rossi and his latter-day Inquisition, *Cavallo Nero*, the Black Knights. Thus, a link between Ryan, Pilgrim, and Cardinal Rossi.

Third, the same treasure-seeking couple are also observed at an antiquarian bookstore in Paris shortly before its owner was murdered by Rossi's operative, and finally Ryan and Pilgrim are killed while diving off Bimini, while the elder Noble was playing golf only a few miles farther south on Cat Cay. Thus, an indistinct and tenuous but very real link between Guzman the drug lord, Noble the pharmaceutical king, and Lord Pilgrim and his girlfriend is established.

The last piece of the puzzle had only been received the night before. One of his well-oiled sources within the CIA had informed him that the Cuban Desk was reporting that Arkady Tomas Cruz, the regime's only known submarine captain, supposedly attached to the Marina de Guerra Revolucionaria, the Revolutionary Navy, as an advisor, was seen boarding an Air Canada flight for Toronto, Canada. The only reason for a Cuban military officer to go to Canada was at the behest of the Military Intelligence Headquarters at the embassy in Ottawa, and presumably that was where this Arkady Cruz individual was going. Kessler had never heard of Cruz, but for many years there had been a persistent although unsubstantiated rumor about the "Lost Cuban Submarine" hidden in the belly of an old freighter, like something from an old James Bond movie. It had always sounded absurd to him, but now Kessler wasn't so sure.

After the drug scandal that led to the execution of Générale Arnaldo Ochoa of the army in 1989, it wasn't hard to make a connection between Angel Guzman's cocaine and heroin army and the Cuban military. Suddenly, using an old submarine for transport wasn't such a stretch of the imagination. It was an intuitive leap to make a connection between Cruz and all the rest of it, but the accuracy of those leaps was what had made Max Kessler a success. He picked up the last crumbs of the pastry with his fork, mashing them delicately before sliding the fork between his lips. He took a sip of coffee and nodded to himself. There was only one conclusion: It looked very much as though there was going to be a rumble in the jungle.

14

At the end of the fifteenth century, Cabo Catoche was at the end of the world; in fact, beyond it. A few years later a Spanish galleon was shipwrecked there, and a few years after that a ship finally anchored there on purpose, the expedition headed by one Francisco Hernández de Córdoba, with a mandate from the governor of Cuba to find slaves for the local sugarcane plantations.

Not surprisingly the locals didn't take too kindly to enslavement and fought back, but their slings, bows, and padded cotton armor were no match for Spanish muskets, cross-bows, and swords. Spaniards one, Mayans zero, including the pillaging of some gold and copper idols plundered from their temple by the Spanish Brother González, a Dominican, and effectively the Inquisition's "political officer" on the voyage, fully capable of deeming any natives or even Spaniards heretics, and ordering them tied to the stake and burned. A lot of clout for a supposedly humble friar.

Cabo, or Cape, Catoche is the Spanish transliteration of the Mayan word *catoc*, which simply means "our houses," or "our place." It is located on the northernmost tip of the Yucatán Peninsula approximately thirty-three miles north of the resort town of Cancún. Most of the area, once the Mayan province of Ecab, has been totally uninhabited for the past five hundred years and is virtually inaccessible by road or air. In the mid-1990s it was designated as a nature preserve, although some efforts, all of which have failed, have been made to develop the coastal area. The closest place is the nearly abandoned village of Taxmal, a few ragged thatch-roofed huts that was all that remained of a once thriving market town on the edge of the jungle east of Kantunilkin and north of Leona Vicario.

It had taken Finn Ryan almost a month to get there, the speed of light by Mexican bureaucratic standards. The fact that her father and mother had been well-known archaeologists in the Yucatán speeded things up a little, and so did her own background. The media coverage she'd received from her previous exploits recovering stolen Nazi art and her recent adventures in the South China Sea didn't hurt either. She and Billy spent two weeks in Miami equipping themselves for a jungle expedition, then crossed the Gulf of Mexico and dropped anchor in the old port town of Progreso.

They left Run-Run McSeveney to his own happily obscure devices on board the *Hispaniola* along with Briney Hanson, and hired a truck to take them and their equipment into the nearby city of Merida, the capital of Yucatán province. They spent another week in Merida at the local Hilton, organizing last-minute permits, then headed off in several rented Toyota Land Cruisers on the overland trip to Taxmal.

There they had arranged to meet their so-called archaeological consultant and their escort. The archaeological consultant was usually an official from the Instituto Nacional de Antropología e Historia, which, from Finn's experience, meant a quasi-cop attached to the expedition to make sure that the gringos weren't tomb robbers out to discover a hoard of pre-Columbian art to smuggle back to the voracious buyers in New York and L.A.

The escort usually consisted of at least a couple of members of the Mexican army. They were inevitably irritating, but considering the past history of Americans and other outsiders stealing their cultural patrimony, the safeguards were reasonable enough. The armed guards could actually come in handy if they ran into trouble in the jungle—banditos and druggies of one kind or another were an inevitable part of doing archaeological business in Mexico these days, especially when you went off the beaten track the way they were about to.

"So, where is this Dr. Garza we're supposed to meet?" Eli Santoro asked, standing by the lead Land Cruiser and looking around at what passed for the main square of the village. Dr. Ruben Filiberto Garza was the consultant attached to the expedition by the National Institute and he was nowhere to be seen. A yellow dog padded across the dusty square and disappeared behind a small house covered in faded pink adobe. The windows of the house were like blind, black holes and the front door was wide open. At the far side of the square the narrow dirt road they had driven into town on faded into the dark jungle canopy beyond.

"He's not here," said Guido Derlagen, looking around.

"Nobody is," said Billy Pilgrim. From the distance came an echoing, hammering sound followed by something that sounded like a human shriek of pain.

"Dear God," whispered Guido, a look of horror twitching across his face at the sudden tortured sound. "Someone is being murdered, I think."

"Golden-fronted woodpecker—*Melanerpes aurifrons*," said Finn. "The scream was from a great-tailed grackle— *Quiscalus mexicanus*."

"Really?" Billy grinned, looking at his friend.

"Really," answered Finn. "I spent entire summers in these jungles when I was a kid. Mom was quite the bird-watcher. I hated them."

"Then why learn their songs and Latin names?"

"Had to do something after my Barbies got eaten by the kinkajous and my *Wonder Woman* comics came down with terminal mildew." Finn shrugged. "It was osmosis, I guess. You learn about things without even knowing you're learning. Or wanting to."

"Zwarte Peiten," said Guido.

"Who?" Eli Santoro asked.

"Black Pete, Sinter Klaas's helper. He is from Spain. If you are in Zwarte Peiten's logbook you are sent to Spain and disappear like the Lost Boys in your Peter Pan story. Very politically incorrect in Holland these days. Now he is called Groen Peiten, Blauw Peiten, Oraje Peiten, even Paars Peiten, anything but Black Pete. It is very sad."

"What in God's name are you talking about?" Billy asked, staring.

"My father is a retired professor of languages from the University of Leiden," explained the Dutchman. "He has written entire books on the whole concept of the Zwarte Peiten. Ruined Christmas for me, I can tell you. It is the same as Finn's birds. I know more about Zwarte Peiten than I ever wanted to." The tall, shaved-headed man sighed. "All I really wanted was a few cookies and candies in my wooden shoe." Off in the jungle, *Quiscalus mexicanus* screamed again.

"That still doesn't answer the question," said Eli. "Where's the tour guide and his buddies?"

"We can't leave without him," said Finn, the irritation rising in her voice. "They'd revoke our permits in a flash."

In the distance there was the whickering sound of an approaching helicopter. Squinting, Billy shaded his eyes with one hand and looked up into the sunlit sky. The thumping of the rotors heightened.

"I think our tour guide is about to make his entrance," murmured Billy. The chopper came in from behind them, a huge thundering insect in jungle camouflage and marked with the triangular red, white, and green roundel of the Mexican air force. It was an old-fashioned UH-1 Iroquois, the ubiquitous Huey, a relic of the sixties and still one of the most potent symbols of the Vietnam War.

The big blunt-nosed machine dropped down into the empty square, tearing patches of thatch from the roofs of the empty huts and rattling the few remaining shutters on the windows as its rotors slowed. Dust blew outward in a blinding whirlwind that raged and eddied while the sliding door in the side of the helicopter slammed back on its runners even before the machine set down. Half a dozen men poured out, all of them armed, all in jungle fatigues, all with machetes on their belts and all wearing floppy boonie hats and wrap-around sunglasses. Each man carried a huge pack on his back and gripped a heavy camouflaged equipment bag in his left hand.

The last man stepped down. He was older than the others, bareheaded with iron gray hair. He was wearing a bright yellow nylon jacket, faintly military-looking cargo pants, and hiking boots. All the men ducked under the rotors and headed toward Finn and the others. The helicopter waited until they were well away, then angled up into the sky with a roar and headed back the way it had come.

The six men in uniform ranged up into a single line and the man in the yellow jacket stepped forward. He had hard, dark, and intelligent eyes and a face the color of old mahogany, pocked and marked like the surface of the moon. It looked as though someone had dragged him behind a moving vehicle face-first along a gravel road. He had a hooked nose and thin lips. When he smiled his teeth gleamed whitely out of the horror of his face.

"My name is Professor Ruben Filiberto Garza," he said. "I am your archaeological consultant." His English was perfect and almost without accent. "These men are from the Grupo Aeromóvil de Fuerzas Especiales del Alto Mando, the Airborne Special Forces." His smile broadened without the faintest hint of humor. Garza stared at Finn as though she was naked. "Think of them as your Navy SEALs, but without the water." He made the slightest attempt at a bow. "You are Miss Ryan, I presume."

Finn nodded, trying to keep herself from staring too hard at the ruin of the man's face. "That's right," she said.

Garza looked at Billy. "That would make you Mr. Pilgrim then."

"It's Lord Pilgrim actually, Dr. Garza," said Billy mildly. "Baron of Neath, Earl of Pendennis, Duke of Kernow and all the rest of it, but I don't stand on ceremony about such things. Just call me William, if you like."

He stepped forward with his hand extended. Garza stared at it as though he was being offered a poisonous snake.

Finn fought off a smile. Watching Billy put people in their place was a treat sometimes.

"I understand you have some familiarity with this part of the world, Miss Ryan," said Garza, ignoring Billy and concentrating on Finn.

She nodded.

The half dozen soldiers behind Garza unlimbered their machetes from their canvas scabbards and waited, their expressions blank behind their sunglasses.

"You will be aware then that we have a number of poisonous snakes in the region, including terciopelo, the fer-de-lance?"

"*Bothrops asper*," answered Finn promptly. "The pit viper." She smiled. "The females are the more dangerous of the species, and the larger, growing up to four feet or so. I've seen a few. Their venom causes immediate necrosis, like flesh-eating disease. The other one to watch out for is *Crotalus durissus*, the cascabel, or South American rattlesnake. I've seen a few of those as well. If we were closer to the coast I might worry about the coral snake, but we're not in their normal range here."

"Why doesn't she ever mention this sort of thing before we start out on these wild-goose chases?" whispered Billy to Guido.

"We might also run into the Mexican beaded lizard *Heloderma horridum*," added Finn. "They can kill you too. Not to mention scorpions, black widows, African killer bees, and agua mala. Jungles are scary places, Dr. Garza. I'm aware of that fact."

"I hope she is also aware that there are seven of them against four of us," murmured Guido, looking at the gleaming machetes in the hands of the soldiers.

"It's good to know you are familiar with these things," said Garza. "The Yucatán is not a place for naiveté. We're a long way from Cancún and Cozumel."

"And we're a long way from our destinations, Doctor, so perhaps we should begin the journey."

"Just so long as you know what you are getting into," cautioned Garza.

"This is a survey mission, Dr. Garza," answered Finn. "We're not here to raid tombs or steal artifacts. We have data that would indicate the existence of a major site, and the remote-sensing information, LANSAT satellite thermal imagery, and geophysics confirm it. We have GPS coordinates showing a hitherto unexplored anomaly seventy-three miles almost due north of here, thirty miles west of the old sisal plantation called Rancho Porvenir."

"Hitherto unexplored anomaly?" Billy whispered. "That's really quite good."

"So," said Garza. "Which way should we go?"

Finn reached into the pack at her feet and took out a handheld Garmin GPS unit and switched it on. She looked at it, then pointed down the roadway that vanished into the jungle on the far side of the abandoned village.

"That way."

Garza barked an order and the soldiers formed up into three pairs of two, two pairs in front, one pair in back with Garza, and Finn's people in between. They moved off.

"Why is the village empty?" Finn asked as they headed down the dusty track toward the darker jungle canopy.

"They found employment elsewhere."

"Farming?"

"Working for the *cocainistas* in the area. It pays better than growing a few stunted patches of maize. The curse of the Yucatán, I'm afraid." He made an even uglier face than his usual one. "Not all of us can work serving mojitos to the gringo tourists at the Cancún Hilton."

Finn ignored the comment, although she sympathized. Cancún was to Mexico as Disney World was to the back alleys of downtown Detroit.

"Are we likely to run into any of these *cocainistas*, as you call them?"

Garza smiled. "My men certainly hope so," he said and laughed.

"I'm not looking for any trouble, Doctor."

"*Acocote nuevo, tlachiquero viejo*," said Garza.

"Huh?" Eli said.

166

"It's a tough job but someone's got to do it," translated Billy.

"Very good, Your Lordship," said Garza, his tone mocking.

"*Muchas gracias, Catedrático* Garza," replied Billy with an equally mocking bow.

Garza scowled.

Finn sighed. This wasn't going the way she'd hoped.

They reached the end of the path and the huge ceiba trees that marked the edge of the village. Finn took a last look back. The yellow dog they'd seen when they arrived in the village was sitting on its skinny haunches in the middle of the deserted square, staring back at her. It barked once, then got up, shook itself, and wandered away. Finn stepped off the end of the track and the jungle swallowed her whole.

15

There were a thousand rooms within the Vatican where meetings could be held, each and every one of them under some kind of surveillance by the Servizio Informazioni del Vaticano, the Vatican Secret Service, best known for its embarrassing and completely false investigation of a religiously oriented UFO phenomenon, which later turned out to be a conspiracy theory launched by an Italian journalist living in Rome with too much time on his hands and his tongue firmly in his cheek.

By the time the laughter subsided the SIV had its cover blown for good, but no one took them very seriously. No one, that is, except the people inside the Vatican who knew better, Cardinal Enrico Rossi of the *Cavallo Nero* among them. As a consequence, any meetings of the secret group were held at a vacant convent just outside the small religious town of Subiaco, some twenty-five miles from Rome.

The town was best known for being the place where the Benedictine order was established, although interestingly enough some of its other famous one-time residents included Lucretia Borgia, the famed poisoner, and Gina Lollobrigida, the film star. While everyone's activities within the Vatican were monitored, it was almost impossible to keep track of anyone in the crowded tourist town.

The group, known among themselves as the Twelve, came from all walks of life, from high-ranking members of the Church, like Rossi, to industrialists, politicians, communications moguls, and in one case a senior member of the Mafia. They had only two things in common: their fanatical devotion to the ancient form of Catholicism they espoused and an equally fanatical quest for ultimate power.

At this particular meeting there were only five members of the ruling council of the order present, the fewest number able to reach a command decision under the ancient bylaws of *Cavallo Nero.*

The five men were Enrico Rossi; Karl Hoffer from the Banco Venizia, the firm used by the Twelve for their covert expenses; Michael Fabrizio, a New York businessman and a Knight of Malta as well as one of the Twelve, better known in the American press as Mickey Rice; Sean O'Keefe, a longtime armorer for the supposedly defunct Irish Republican Army and now an independent and perfectly legitimate arms dealer living in Rome; and finally, Father Manuel Pérez, once the head of the Colombian Ejército de Liberación Nacional, the ELN, or National Liberation Army of that country.

"El Cura Pérez," or Pérez the Priest, had supposedly died of hepatitis in 1998, but in reality he had been living in exile for the last decade acting as liaison between the forces of the Twelve and his colleagues in the ELN. Pérez was the Twelve's central representative for all of South America and provided a great deal of financial aid to the organization.

They met in a cavernous room in the convent that had once been the refectory, empty of furniture except for a long monks table with bench seating accommodating up to twenty people.

"The situation in Mexico has changed somewhat," said Rossi without preamble. He was seated at the head of the table. "Too many cooks are definitely spoiling the broth."

"You'd better explain that, Eminence," said Hoffer, the banker.

"Guzman has become too greedy."

"I told you he'd be trouble," grunted Pérez, a thin gray-haired man in the garb of an ordinary priest.

"He's no trouble," said O'Keefe with a laugh. "He's just mad as a bloody hatter, he is."

"Mad or greedy, it makes no difference. He must be dealt with," said Rossi.

"Exactly what form has this greed taken?" Mickey Rice asked, cutting to the heart of the matter.

"He's involved the Cubans."

"Feck! He's crazier than I thought," breathed O'Keefe.

"How does this affect our deal with the Nobles?" Mickey Rice asked.

"That's another matter. The two are connected, clearly, and the younger Noble has decided to take on the Ryan woman and her friend on his own."

"A little initiative, is it?" O'Keefe said.

Rossi frowned. "The Nobles are very high-profile. So is the Ryan woman. On two occasions now our paths have crossed, to our great loss, I might add."

"So deal with them," said Hoffer.

"And if the Nobles interfere?" Rossi snorted. "Noble Pharmaceuticals represents a huge investment for us at the moment."

"And I've got a lot riding on them myself," said Rice.

"We are in a very delicate position, playing Guzman off against the others. If we act precipitously we may wind up shooting ourselves in the foot," said Rossi.

"Then you'd better find a better shooter," said O'Keefe.

"My thoughts exactly." Rossi nodded.

"The young man you used in Paris?" Hoffer asked curiously.

"No," said Rossi. "Competent, but good only in urban situations, I would think." The cardinal shook his head. "I have someone else in mind." The cardinal smiled briefly. "An old soldier. One of our best."

His name was Francis Xavier Sears, just like the department stores. Born in 1949, Francis Sears volunteered for the United States Army on his eighteenth birthday. After basic training at Fort Benning, Georgia, he was sent to Vietnam as a member of Charlie Company of 1st Battalion, 20th Infantry Regiment, 11th Brigade, 23rd Infantry Division.

Attached to several platoons during his first tour, Francis thrived. He was noted by several officers as being totally fearless and often volunteered for the most dangerous assignments and patrols. His first platoon leader, a captain named Rigby, was on record as saying that Francis seemed to have "a splendid appetite for killing."

Achieving the rank of sergeant, he was eventually noticed by a Special Forces recruiter named Wizner. Wizner in turn handed him over to a Central Intelligence advisor named Joe Currie, who introduced him to the Phoenix Program. Murder in Phoenix was a recreation, a way of life, a family tradition that had nothing at all to do with ideology, north or south. Heads were collected like bowling trophies.

There was another man after that, someone more remote than Wizner with the unlikely name of T. Fox Grimaldi. He said that he was a distant relation of Princess Grace's husband, but Francis doubted that—more likely he was a descendant of a pizza chef from New Jersey. T.

Fox Grimaldi had a club foot and a built-up shoe. He wore Brooks Brothers suits and thin suede ties. He looked like a rodent of some kind and had a five o'clock shadow that made him look like a liar, which he was. Francis discovered a long time later that his first name was Tim, and that was the reason he only ever used the initial.

T. Fox Grimaldi used Francis long after the end of the war. Grimaldi ran the infamous Blowback Boys, kept on in Saigon after the fall to take out old allies left behind who knew too much. Embarrassments. Blowback took its toll and by the end of it Francis was the only one left alive. Almost a legend, on his way to becoming a myth. By then even he was aware that he was something less than human, but at the same time something more. When Blowback was finally over, T. Fox Grimaldi brought Francis Sears home. Grimaldi retired from the CIA, or most likely was retired *by* them.

Whatever the case, he kept up his relationship with Sears and used him regularly for contract jobs with a number of clients in the private sector. One of those clients was *Cavallo Nero*, and on the sudden and somewhat mysterious death of Grimaldi in the late '90s, Sears began to contract himself out. He had done more than satisfactory work for the Twelve in the past.

At the present he was in the main square of Scobie, Indiana, the capital of Duchess County in the extreme southern portion of the state. Scobie had a population of a little over twelve thousand, many of them of German descent. The main industry in the small city was the manufacture of wood furniture, as well as education, Scobie being the home of a campus of Duchess College. It was also the hometown of Bishop Terrence Boucher. The bishop, who normally lived in Fort Wayne, where he taught history and was the headmaster of a local prep school, was back in Scobie to care for his dying mother. The bishop was a pedophile.

Also in Scobie was a young man named William Huggins. Huggins, an ambulance driver and a devout Catholic, had privately mentioned his experiences with the bishop and announced his intention to make his abuse public. Unfortunately for Huggins, the "friend" he had mentioned the bishop's predilections to was a low-level agent for *Cavallo Nero*. That agent had passed the information on to New York, which in turn had sent the information to Cardinal Rossi. The cardinal was already aware of Boucher's sexual preferences. He was also aware that Boucher, who had once worked for the Vatican secretary of state's office, a position Rossi had occupied at the time, knew of *Cavallo Nero* and would use that knowledge in an attempt to barter his way out of any charges brought against him. This, Rossi knew, could not be allowed to happen. Sears had been dispatched to deal with it.

Francis Xavier Sears sat on a bench in the town square, the Jeffersonian county courthouse at his back. He was doing one of his favorite things as he sat enjoying the midday sun. He was thinking about murder, something he knew a great deal about. Killing was easy, of course. You could do it effectively with everything from a long-range sniper rifle to a piece of broken brick.

Any hand tool on a carpenter's bench had been used as a murder weapon once upon a time, as had every utensil in the average kitchen. But that kind of killing took no skill, had no style, and lacked finesse. Not to mention that most killers stupid enough to use a brick to bash someone's brains were usually stupid enough to get caught.

On the other hand, with a moderate level of intelligence and skill, getting away with murder was relatively easy. Despite *CSI, Law and Order,* and all their various incarnations, television was not reality. A district attorney offered half a fingerprint and a scratch of paint from a passing car wasn't likely to bring a case to trial. The truth about forensics had more to do with overworked departments and underpaid staff than it did with glossy labs and quirky bosses collecting bugs. All you had to do was remember the O.J. Simpson trial for proof of that. The prosecution of murder was a matter of money and bureaucracy. Avoid those and you were home free. The best way to commit murder, of course, was to give a cop even the vaguest opportunity to convince himself that the corpse in front of his face was caused either accidentally or by the corpse's own hand.

There were fifteen members of the local Scobie Police Department, twelve members of the Duchess County Sheriff's Department, and thirty-four members of the district office of the Indiana State Police. The nearest forensic lab was in Indianapolis. That came out to sixty-four law enforcement officers across three eight-hour shifts.

Of all of those there were only three full-time investigating officers. There was more money in the budget for trash burning violations than there was for violent crime. According to the statistics he'd read in the *Duchess County Leader Post* there had been only three murders in Duchess County in the last ten years, all of them a result of domestic violence. On the other hand, there had been more than two hundred and ninety accidental deaths in the same time period. It was more than likely that the bishop was about to become the victim of a tragic mishap. Either that or he was going to die suddenly from natural causes.

Disregarding automobile wrecks, there were roughly a hundred thousand fatalities from accidents in the United States every year. Of those the majority came from machine accidents, falls, drowning, and suffocation, in that order. There were no large bodies of water nearby for the bishop to drown in, and besides, Sears's research indicated that the cleric was a powerful swimmer, even at the age of sixty-nine. Given his occupation, there was also little chance of a death by machinery, which ruled that out as well. Suffocation was always a good bet, but in this case it would be difficult to arrange.

Realistically it would have to be a fall. The question was, from where? Indiana was basically as flat as an IHOP waffle. There were several nearby limestone quarries and some tourist caves, but why would a Catholic bishop with a dying mother go to either place?

The options were narrowing. The last time Boucher had visited his mother, Francis Xavier had done a quick reconnaissance of the dying woman's home. It was the home Boucher had grown up in, a modest place. It was small, one and a half stories, with two bedrooms and a bathroom in an upstairs dormer, and a living room, dining room, back kitchen, and what passed for a den or study on the ground floor. A single flight of stairs led from the upper level to the lower. There was no landing. The hardwood steps were covered with an old paisley runner held taut with brass rails.

It really was the only way. A little on the dangerous side since he'd have to be on the scene to remove the evidence, however. The key to it all, of course, was the fact that there was no landing and no padding under the runner. Francis Xavier estimated the bishop's height as not quite six feet and his weight at something over one hundred and eighty-five pounds. A fall down thirteen steps to the uncarpeted foyer at the front entrance would almost surely break the man's neck, and if it didn't quite do it, Sears would be there to finish the job.

He looked across Courthouse Square and read the old-fashioned sign on the window of the store on the corner: JOSEF KORZENIOWSKI; HARDWARE, STOVES & TINWARE—SINCE 1924. It was the kind of classic place that you'd find in a Ray Bradbury story, full of interesting and potentially lethal items. They'd have everything Francis Xavier needed.

He glanced upward. Above the store there were windows in the redbrick building. A curious crossing of the fates. The three windows belonged to the small apartment occupied by Huggins, the potential whistleblower. Huggins would be easy, though. He drank too much and everyone knew he had high blood pressure.

Twenty cc's of insulin delivered by a twenty-five-gauge needle inserted into the posterior auricular artery under the jaw would deliver enough of the drug to instantly cause a fatal stroke. Personal observation told Sears that his intended victim had poor skin, was prone to razor burn, and had large, rather oily pores. Even if, for some reason, the medical examiner ordered an autopsy, the needle insertion point would be virtually invisible and the insulin levels would have long since dissipated. Not a perfect murder by any means, but under the circumstances and in this environment, not far from it. There was nothing to connect the deaths of an ambulance attendant who had once been an altar boy to a simple parish priest more than forty years ago and an aging bishop who'd sadly fallen down the stairs in his mother's house. Problem solved.

Francis Xavier Sears put his head back, closed his eyes, and enjoyed the warmth of the sun on his face, listening to the sounds of small-town life go on around him, the soft breeze rustling the leaves of the maple trees in the square. Death was good, but sometimes life was even better.

16

It was almost midnight. The *Noble Dancer*, all sleek 189 feet of her, rode easily in the small chop that ruffled the waters of the Gulf of Mexico. The yacht had four decks, its own elevator, and accommodations for up to twenty-five people, including crew. She was powered by two fifteen-hundred-horsepower Caterpillar engines and could achieve speeds of up to eighteen knots.

The massive ship was outfitted for almost anything, including cross-ocean ventures. Her amenities included every kind of electronic toy, "zero speed" stabilizers that gave the vessel enough stability to allow competition billiards in the dedicated games room, a Jacuzzi, a sun-deck, and a baby grand piano. The yacht was a plaything for a billionaire.

The dining room looked as though it had come out of a Hollywood mansion, complete with cabinets full of crystal, Persian carpets on the deck, and an immense rosewood dining table able to seat fifteen guests. Tonight, instead of a sumptuous midnight snack, the table was set for armed combat. Military gear was spread out on the shining, heavily varnished marquetry from one end to the other.

Four members of the incursion team were checking their weapons and survival equipment. They had the hard, practiced look of professional soldiers, which all of them had been at one time or another.

All of them were dressed in jungle fatigues and none of the dappled uniforms showed any sign of rank. All had a small badge on the left breast pocket of their blouses that showed a black hawk on a yellow ground, piped in red.

The symbol had been James Jonas Noble's single conceit when he formed the security company to protect his many interests around the world. As a boy growing up during the war, Blackhawk Comics had been his favorite, so he had adopted the Blackhawk symbol as the logo for the company of the same name.

Blackhawk Security Consultants had originally been intended as a private security force for Noble Pharmaceuticals, but it had been organized at a time when the use of contracted paramilitary groups was on the rise, and as a consequence the company had grown far outside the limits of a simple security force to guard Noble facilities.

Based in Georgia, it had a huge training facility and offices in every major country in the world, as well as several minor ones. Much of its business was concentrated in Africa, the Middle East, and Central America, including Mexico, where the company provided body-guards, transportation, and intelligence to foreign embassy personnel, as well as a number of high-ranking Mexican government officials.

The four-man team now aboard the *Noble Dancer* were all Spanish-speaking and in previous lives had all taken part in at least one revolution or insurrection in jungle conditions. The leader of the group, Tibor Cherka, a tall, grizzled American in his fifties, had been a member of one of the first incursion teams in Panama and before that had supposedly worked closely with the National Guard's so-called death squads in El Salvador, although nothing was ever proven. As Cherka's men prepared themselves in the dining room, Harrison Noble had a final meeting with his father in the pilot-house, one deck above.

"I still don't approve," said the elder Noble, staring out into the darkness. "Let Cherka do it—he's a professional."

"I'm not saying he doesn't know his job," said the younger man. "I'm just saying that beyond the military aspects he doesn't know what to look for. I do."

"True enough," said Noble senior.

"He's got enough weaponry to fight a small war—that part of it I'll leave up to him—but I've got to be on-site first. You know that, Father."

"And if things go wrong?"

"They won't," said Harrison Noble. "I guarantee it."

The older man turned to his son, his features grimly set.

"Where have I heard that before? Screw this up and we're all going to take the fall—you realize that, I hope."

"Of course."

"Not a word of this can leak out and you can't be squeamish. If it all starts to go south, get out of there, but not before you clean up after yourself. No mercy. No survivors. No mistakes like last time."

"I realize that, Father."

"You know the plan?"

It was the tenth time they'd gone over it since the *Noble Dancer* had left Miami. Harrison Noble sighed. Sometimes the old man was a right royal pain.

"Yes, I know the plan."

The *Noble Dancer* presently stood fifteen miles off the coast, three miles outside Mexican territorial waters. At high tide, in just less than an hour, the yacht would come in three miles to the exact GPS limit and launch the two GTX three-passenger Sea-Doos from the platform on the upper deck where they were presently waiting.

The high-speed jetboats easily had at least an hour of running time at top speed, a solid fifty miles an hour. Cherka, the team leader, estimated they'd reach the beach just east of the small fishing village of El Cuyo at something under ten minutes. The Sea-Doos would then be scuttled offshore to prevent discovery.

If the Nobles' latest information from Max Kessler was correct, traveling on foot from the village to their destination was expected to take two full days through the tropical rain forest that lay on the edge of the Rio Lagartos National Park, at least twenty-four hours ahead of Finn Ryan and her little inland expedition. Once on-site, Harrison junior would complete his investigation of the temple and the surrounding area, hopefully killing two birds with one stone.

With the job accomplished, one way or another the team would rendezvous at a preselected GPS coordinate outside the tiny village of San Angel, where they would be exfiltrated by a Blackhawk Security Bell JetRanger helicopter in civilian livery, probably that of a fictitious helitour company. From San Angel, their gear abandoned, they would be flown to Isla Mujeres off the coast, where they would then board the *Noble Dancer*, now legitimately berthed in the local marina.

Forty minutes after the conversation, Harrison Noble, now dressed in a roomy, dark blue dry suit over his jungle fatigues, boarded one of the pair of heavy, unmarked jet-black Sea-Doos winched down into the sea beside the gently swaying yacht. Cherka, in the lead Sea-Doo, gave the signal, and the two-hundred-fifteen-horsepower Rotex engines burst into life, the jet pumps spitting out a burbling stream of water.

Cherka, two of his heavily equipped men on the molded seats behind him, clicked the transmission into Forward, twisted the throttle hard, and headed for the invisible coast a dozen miles away. On the second water-craft, Harrison Noble, with a single passenger and more equipment loaded behind him, turned his own throttle and followed.

William Hartley Mossberg, Special Assistant to the Assistant Deputy National Security Advisor to the President of the United States, was late. He stepped out of his broom-closet office next to the lobby in the West Wing of the White House and then walked out through the canopied side entrance to the street, a section of Executive Avenue closed off to anything but White House traffic and effectively turned into a parking lot.

He looked at his watch. It was a fifty-dollar Indiglo with the stars and stripes on the dial, just like the one stolen from the president on his last trip to Albania. Prior to purchasing the light-'em-up Indiglo he'd worn a six-thousand-dollar Patek Philippe knockoff that was a twin to the sixty-grand original one the president of Russia wore, but the president had noticed it in passing one day and told him to get rid of it since it made him look like a "Jewish banker." Thankfully there had been no one nearby to hear the ill-advised and unfortunate comment, but Mossberg got rid of the knockoff and picked up the hard-to-find commemorative Indiglo on E-bay. So far Tumbleweed, as the Secret Service code-named his imperial prezship, hadn't noticed, but you never knew. Ambassadorships had been handed out for less. Through devious old-boy back channels Mossberg had learned that he'd been hired on the basis that his name reminded Tumbleweed of the shotgun manufacturer and not, as he'd initially presumed, because he'd gone to Yale, graduating 1,287th out of a class of 1,400.

In the end, of course, William Hartley Mossberg couldn't have cared less how he'd reached the White House; the fact was he had arrived there and he was going to do his best to stay. All he had was a lousy master of studies in law degree, but after four years in the White House it would easily be enough to get him some kind of nonlawyer schmooze job at a big firm in Fort Smith, and failing that he could run for any office he wanted in his hometown of Arkadelphia. Best of all, if he could somehow swing it he might even be able to land something here in D.C. as a junior lobbyist. Which was why it didn't do to be late for a late-night meeting with Max Kessler.

Mossberg reached the end of West Executive Avenue, picked up a cab outside the security booth, and gave the driver the address for Harry's Saloon at Eleventh and Pennsylvania. He could think of other places he could be heading for at this time of night, Apex in particular, up on Dupont Circle. But that was another story, one that had gotten him into the trouble he was in and another very good reason for saying, "How high?" when Max Kessler said, "Jump."

The cab took a turn around Lafayette Park, came back out onto Pennsylvania Avenue beyond the eastern security barrier, and headed toward Eleventh. Harry's was located in an office building directly across from the ESPN Zone sports bar and catercorner to the Old Post Office Building, now gutted and turned into an upscale shopping mall.

The cab let him out on Pennsylvania Avenue and he turned the corner onto Eleventh. He pushed through the door and stepped into the long, high-ceilinged room. It was still going strong even after midnight, populated mainly by tourists and people who'd just come out of the Warner Theater down the street.

Kessler, alone as always, was seated at a table halfway down the room, fastidiously eating a dripping hamburger with a napkin tucked into his collar. He was watching the CNN roller on one of the half dozen televisions set high above the long bar. There was no sound. Even if the volume had been turned up it would have remained unheard over the steady humming din of the patrons. It was a lesson Kessler had explained to him shortly after they first met: a noisy room was a secure one. If everyone else was talking it meant that no one else was listening to you.

"I had them put some blue cheese dressing on the hamburger. It's quite good actually— you should try one. Fry?" Kessler asked, holding up a crispy length of potato.

"No, thanks," said Mossberg, cringing slightly. It occurred to him that at every meeting he'd had with the ugly little man, Max Kessler had been eating. He had an oddly obscene habit of dabbing at his lips too often with his napkin, and inevitably cleared his throat after each dab. He looked like a gigantic spider eating flies.

A waitress appeared. Mossberg ordered a Zhujiang lager, which was about as exotic as it got for Harry's.

"So," said Kessler after the waitress faded away, "how are we tonight?"

"As well as can be expected, under the circumstances."

"You still think I'm blackmailing you?" Kessler smiled. He used a steak knife to carve a sliver from his open-faced burger and popped it into his mouth. Kessler was the only person William Hartley Mossberg had ever seen who could smile and chew simultaneously.

"I don't know what else you'd call it," the young man said. His beer arrived along with a pilsner glass. He poured and took a long, sharp swallow. It didn't do any good at all.

Kessler swallowed. Somehow, two years ago the little ferret had discovered that William Hartley was a regular at Apex and a variety of other gay clubs in Washington, including the notorious Lizard Lounge. D.C. had always been relatively tolerant of sexual predilections of virtually any stripe, but with a hard-line Republican in the Oval Office and tales of airport washroom two-steps abounding, it didn't do to flaunt it. If William Hartley had been discreet it probably would have been overlooked, but his current main squeeze was a studly fellow on the second floor of the West Wing named Dan Sullivan, an intern in the Communications Office.

Even that might have passed muster in this day and age except for the fact that Daniel was the grandnephew of the current vice president, and that would not do, no indeedy. Monica Lewinsky wasn't related to anyone in the White House, and look at the trouble she'd caused. A sex scandal of this particular type in this particular White House would be a barn burner, with William Hartley trapped inside the barn as it went up in flames.

Kessler stared at the young man across the table from him, dabbed his lips, and sighed.

"I've explained to you before, Will. The information I have is merely a source of leverage. If I was ever to disclose it, lives would be ruined and careers overturned for no good reason. I see our relationship as potentially a mutual one. Don't forget, I'm a supplier of information as well as a collector of it. Intelligence works both ways. There may come a time when I can help you as much as I can hurt you."

"So you've told me on a number of occasions," grumbled Mossberg.

"And meant it each and every time." Kessler paused, surgically attacked his hamburger, and ate another bite. He dabbed his lips again. "Tell me something," he murmured.

"If I can."

"How many satellites are there over Mexico?"

"Ours?"

"Yes."

Mossberg thought about it for a while, sipping his beer. Kessler ate, dabbed, ate and dabbed again. Mossberg finally answered.

"A bunch. A couple of Geos birds, SeaSat, a NASA orbiter for telemetry. The DEA has at least two in conjunction with its AWACS program. There's a Joint Intelligence Lacrosse Onyx put up by the National Reconnaissance Office that swings over Mexico when it's tasked for it."

"What can it do?"

"Anything. It uses something called Synthetic Aperture Radar. Sees through cloud cover. Press the right buttons and it can see under the ground. They call it the Bunker Hunter."

"What would it take to task it for southern Mexico?"

"An intelligence directive."

"How difficult is that for you?"

"As long as it's not some kind of National Security thing, it wouldn't be too difficult. A couple of forms to fill out, a phone call or two. It's optimally in a polar orbit so it can see just about anything, anywhere, anytime."

"I need a very close look at a very small piece of jungle. Could you manage that? Pictures?"

"I guess. If I had the right coordinates."

Kessler answered promptly and exactly, referring to no notes.

"Twenty-one degrees twenty-three minutes nineteen-point-three seconds North by eighty-seven degrees forty minutes thirty-four seconds West."

"Why there?"

Kessler smiled blandly. "That, young man, would be telling."

17

Francis Xavier Spears had found William Huggins the ambulance driver in his apartment over the hardware store, drunk as a skunk and passed out in his narrow unmade bed just two hours after he completed his shift at midnight. According to Sears's initial research, Huggins often drank while on the job, and there were a dozen empty cans of Budweiser and an empty bottle of cheap Pavlova vodka on the man's battered old dining room table to give evidence to his continued binge.

Whether Huggins's drinking habits came about as a result of his long-ago abuse by the bishop or for some other reason was irrelevant to Sears; what counted was the man's comatose condition. Not only would Huggins be unaware of and untroubled by Sears's intrusion, but the effect of the insulin would be increased dramatically. Sears checked the time. A quarter to two. Perfect.

The bedroom was a shabby place. There was a cheap chest of drawers, an open stainless steel clothing rack holding several uniforms and some shirts, an upturned plastic milk crate for a bedside table, and an IKEA

Arstid-style table lamp with a broken pull chain replaced by a dangling piece of string. There was nothing hanging on the walls, which were painted a sullen pale tobacco color. There was a blackout curtain over the window that looked out onto the street. The IKEA light was on. The other things on the table included a package of discount Monte Carlo cigarettes, a matchbook from Shooters Bar and Grill on Main Street a block away, and an empty forty of orange-flavored St. Ides malt liquor.

Sears was already wearing surgical gloves. He reached into the pocket of his Windbreaker and removed a loaded NovoLog FlexPen. He unscrewed the cap and, using his left hand, gently eased Huggins's jaw to one side. The man groaned, broke wind, and shuffled his legs but didn't awaken. Sears was pleased to see that Huggins hadn't shaved. The insertion site would be invisible among the heavy beard, the large pores, and the old razor burn. The man had the complexion of a pizza.

Sears dialed the head of the pen up to a maximum sixty-unit dose, gently pinched the skin under Huggins's jaw to find the artery, then inserted the ultrafine needle. Huggins didn't even flinch. Sears kept the needle firmly lodged in the artery for a full six seconds, making sure that all the insulin had been delivered. Finally he withdrew the now-empty pen, screwed on the cap again, and simply stood there, looking down at the innocent victim.

As far as murder was concerned, Sears had learned many years ago that patience was a virtue, a key one if the murder was to remain undetected. The majority of murderers were eventually caught because they rushed the job and left something behind or something undone.

The fact that the death of William Huggins would go unnoticed for a minimum of twelve hours, allowing the scene to decay, was immaterial; care had to be taken, even though his victim's passing would be unremarkable and unremarked on. Even the death of a nobody was important, at least to Sears. So he waited.

NovoLog was a fast-acting insulin, and within ten minutes the first signs of distress became visible as the insulin in his brain put him into hypoglycemic shock as his blood sugar plummeted. A cold sweat broke out on the man's forehead, followed by mild shaking or light convulsions of his arms and legs. Sears reached out and put his finger on the man's carotid. The pulse was frantic as Huggins descended into tachycardia.

He groaned then, his torso convulsing as he began to vomit, choking on it. His eyes flew open then rolled back, showing only the whites. He began to convulse heavily and then, suddenly, everything subsided. Huggins's sphincter loosened and the stink of human waste rose out of the bedclothes. From dead drunk to just plain dead in eleven and a half minutes.

Sears gazed around the room, looking for problems, finding none. He checked himself. None of the man's fluids had reached him. He was already wearing disposable surgical booties and a paper cap. There would be no trace. No suspicion.

He turned away from the fresh corpse and left the room. He walked back through the apartment, touching nothing. The windows here closed, and either Huggins had been too drunk to turn on the air conditioner in the dining room or it didn't work. Either way the apartment would be a furnace by noon. The blowflies would be hard at work by then, the first maggots appearing within six hours.

If nobody checked on the man's whereabouts for a day or two the smell coming down into the hardware store might be the first clue, and by then the corpse would be a terrible mess. Sears gave the room a last once-over and checked his wristwatch. Two a.m. The bars would be emptying out. There'd be lots of people on the street, a crowd to vanish into with the police cruisers probably concentrating on places like Shooters a few blocks to the south beyond Courthouse Square. He'd be an insomniac tourist on the way back to his bed-and-breakfast, a traveling salesman for a medical supply company just like his business card and other ID proclaimed.

He reached the back door, carefully removed the strip of tape he'd used to keep it unlocked, and stepped out onto the wooden stairs that led down to the courtyard loading zone behind the hardware store. He took care not to wipe the existing prints off the doorknob. Wiped areas were dangerous. A smudge or two wouldn't bother anyone, if they even decided to dust for prints at all.

He waited for a moment at the bottom of the steps, peeled off his surgical gloves and the paper booties he'd worn, and put them into his jacket pocket. He walked slowly across the small courtyard and went down a narrow alley, exiting onto Isaac Street. Seeing no one but hearing the echo of some shouts and honking horns from the bar a few blocks away, he went down Isaac Street to Sixth and turned onto Sixth Avenue.

Mrs. Rothwell's bed-and-breakfast was located across from a hulking old redbrick middle school. It was a big old mansard-roof mansion like something out of the *Magnificent Ambersons*. A dozen bedrooms, wood-paneled walls, and worn old carpets on yellow varnished hardwood floors. The furniture was antique or at least trying to be, and there was a rear brick patio and flower beds everywhere. Three of the guest rooms had private baths and Sears had taken one of them. It was on the main floor at the rear, with French doors leading out to the patio, which suited him perfectly.

Sears went to the long narrow parking lot at the side of the building and unlocked the trunk of his Hertz rental. He took out a medium-sized plastic bag, locked the trunk, and went to the far end of the parking lot then followed the property line of the bed-and-breakfast to the rear alley.

He turned right down the dark alley, counting the garages until he reached the old chain-link fence that marked the alley end of the property belonging to the bishop's mother. He stopped then, opened the bag, and took out a can of WD-40 with its wand already attached. He sprayed the hinges of the gate and the slip latch, put the can back into the bag, and stepped into the bishop's backyard. A dog barked a few doors down and he could still hear the distant sounds of car horns, but other than that there was nothing. He checked his watch. Ten past two.

Sears looked up at the rear of the house at three windows on the dormered second floor, two ordinary windows flanking a smaller frosted-glass one in the middle. There was a faint light glowing from the middle room. A nightlight in the bathroom, most likely. Bedrooms on both sides, dark. There were three windows on the main floor as well. All dark. The bishop was in bed, asleep after spending most of the day at the hospital with his dying mother.

Sears slipped across the back lawn and went up onto the narrow back porch. He put the plastic bag down, withdrew another pair of paper booties and a full-body DuPont Tyvek jumpsuit complete with a drawstring hood. He quickly slipped into the suit, put on the booties, and picked up the bag again. He put on a second pair of surgical gloves and found the spare key just where he'd discovered it the night before—on the lintel above the door.

He used the WD-40 again, slid the key into the lock and turned it. The door opened smoothly. He stepped into the bishop's kitchen. He went through the kitchen and down the hall to the foyer by the front door. Creeping silently to the top stairs, he glanced quickly into the empty hallway, then prepared his trap. He stepped softly back downstairs. There was an old-fashioned telephone bench at the end of the hallway. He stood beside the little table and the equally old-fashioned rotary phone.

He waited, listening for any signs of movement. Then he reached into his bag and took out the disposable Cingular cell phone he'd purchased a week ago and so far had never used. He dialed a number. The old phone on the table gave a jangling ring. He could hear the simultaneous ringing of the extension upstairs. He waited. After five rings he heard the froggy, mumbling voice of the bishop, suddenly jarred from sleep. He'd immediately think that it was the hospital calling, telling him of his mother's imminent demise.

"Hello?"

"Come downstairs."

"I beg your pardon?"

"Come downstairs."

"What are you talking about? Who is this? Is this about my mother?"

"Come downstairs."

Sears reached out with one hand and gently picked up the extension, hanging up the cell phone an instant later. There was a dial tone on the old rotary.

"Hello? Hello?"

The upstairs telephone clicked as the bishop hung up. Sears left the rotary off the hook, keeping the line open, just in case. He heard footsteps overhead and a light came on, shining down the stairs. The bishop, in a green silk dressing gown, appeared at the head of the stairs.

"Bishop Boucher." Sears made his voice loud and firm. Commanding. Keeping the man's attention.

"Who the hell are you?" Boucher demanded, blinking, peering through wire-rimmed spectacles. His white hair stood on end. "What do you want?"

"I'm here to talk of sodomy and related matters," said Sears.

"Who the hell do you think you are!? Get out of this house before I phone the police!"

"You shall not be a corrupter of boys, nor like unto such," said Sears pleasantly, keeping his eyes fixed on the old man at the head of the stairs. "The Letter of Barnabus. Not quite scripture, but close enough."

"You bastard!" Boucher roared.

"You pedophile," answered Sears calmly, his eyes taunting.

Bishop Boucher let out a strangled screech. He took a step forward, his bare foot striking the almost invisible piece of fifty-pound test braided monofilament fishing line stretched from one side of the staircase to the other. He pitched forward in a desperate swan dive, arms windmilling in empty air, unable to stop himself. Sears stepped out of the way.

The heavyset man came down headfirst, flailing, striking halfway down. His C7 vertebra snapped with an audible crunch as his neck hit the edge of the hardwood stair at an impossible angle, twisted grotesquely, and then bounced off. He was dead an instant later and flopped limply down the last six stairs, landing at the bottom in an untidy heap.

Carrying his plastic bag, Sears stepped over and around the dead body and climbed to the top of the stairs, carefully stepping over the edge of the tread where the bishop's head had struck, leaving whatever trace there was intact. At the top of the stairs he opened his plastic bag and took out a medium-sized Buck knife to remove the taut, unbroken piece of braided monofilament.

He balled up the fishing line and put it into the bag along with the knife. With that small damning detail taken care of, he went back down the stairs to the foyer. There was no need to check the bishop; his head was bent almost beneath his body. In his case, like that of his long-ago victim, it was unlikely that the body would be discovered for quite some time since visiting hours at the hospital didn't start until noon.

Carrying his bag, Sears turned away, hung up the hall telephone, and went back to the dark kitchen. He stripped off the Tyvek jumpsuit, leaving the gloves and the booties on. He put the jumpsuit in the bag, stepped out onto the back porch and stripped off the booties, putting them in the bag along with the jumpsuit. He used the spare key to lock the door behind him and replaced it on the ledge. The job was done.

He went down the steps and back through the yard and the alley, returning back to the B&B. He slipped through the French doors on the patio and stepped into his room. Without turning on the lights he pulled the curtains across the opening and crossed to the bed. He sat down and checked the luminous dial of his wristwatch. Two twenty-five.

Sears finally stripped off the surgical gloves and dropped them into the plastic bag. He set the alarm on the traveling alarm clock on the bedside table for six. He'd get up then, the plastic bag with his tools stowed in his briefcase, and pause for one of Mrs. Rothwell's excellent bran muffins before he checked out.

He'd be on the road in his rental by six thirty and be on the interstate twelve minutes after that. By eight he'd be at the Louisville, Kentucky, International Airport, where he'd hand in the rental. By nine he'd be aboard the United Express commuter flight to Washington. An hour and a half after that he'd be at Reagan Airport. He'd be home in time for lunch. So far everything was going exactly according to plan.

He kicked off his shoes and put his head back against the headboard. He lifted up his hand and looked at the slightly creped skin behind his knuckles and the thinning web of skin between his thumb and forefinger. He was even beginning to show little darkening spots here and there. Age. He sighed; there was no escaping it, he supposed. He'd have to start slowing down soon; two in one night was just about his limit, and he really did need his sleep.

His cell phone chirped inside the plastic bag. Sears frowned. There was only one person who knew the number for the disposable. He leaned forward and retrieved the flip phone from the plastic bag. He opened the phone and answered the call.

"Yes?"

A familiar voice spoke softly.

"We have an emergency."

18

The Antonov An-26 turboprop, painted in the livery of Cubana Airlines, droned through the sky over the Gulf of Mexico on a straight course to Mexico City. It was three a.m. It was a regularly scheduled cargo flight and, oddly enough, it was almost exactly on time, proceeding on course and procedurally correct in every way, calling in every half hour to Mexico Federal Air Traffic Center and identifying itself.

Several years previously Mexico had become part of WAAS, orchestrated by the United States. WAAS stood for Wide Area Augmentation System, a combination of three satellites, GPS tracking, and five separate ground stations in Mexico City, San Jose del Cabo, Puerto Vallarta, Merida, and Tapachula.

On the surface WAAS was an attempt to coordinate air traffic control in North America, but the system was also covertly attached to the U.S. military AWACS system out of Eglin Air Force Base in Florida and the Drug Enforcement Administration. As one wit at Eglin put it, "With

WAAS in place, if a seagull farts out of line anywhere in the Gulf of Mexico, we'll know about it."

All aircraft flying in the dense WAAS network had to have identifying GPS beacons that squawked on the system. No beacon meant you were a bad guy, and any suspicious flight could be followed as low as twelve feet on existing radar. No more low-flying DC3s cruising at zero altitude delivering bales of marijuana over the Everglades. If the Antonov deviated more than half a mile off its flight plan, course bells would ring in a dozen different places. Flights out of Havana, especially ones in Russian-made planes, were a top priority.

The cargo hold of the aging transport was half filled with pallets of goods that had been rolled up the rear loading ramp and down the ball-bearing conveyor belt to the forward section, then netted down with web belt strapping. The rear section closest to the ramp held six men, all seated on fold-down jump seats on either side of the hull, their heavy packs in the central aisle between them.

The six men were all dressed in black combat fatigues, any exposed skin covered with stripes of dark green camo stick. Five of the men were members of a Chinese army Special Operations Group, *Long Fei Xing*, the Flying Dragon Squad. They were *Zhan Shou*, the Decapitators, specially trained to seek out and kill the command infrastructure of any enemy, beginning at the top.

This particular group, headed by the infamous Wong Fei Hung, had a great deal of experience in jungle fighting, having operated successfully in most of Southeast Asia, the Philippines, and half a dozen African countries as well. The sixth man seated in the hold of the Antonov with the Flying Dragon Squad was Arkady Cruz.

The plan that had put him seventeen thousand feet above the gulf instead of eight hundred feet below the surface had been developed by DGI's Section II-1 division in Havana. Cruz thought the idea was insane, born out of desperation, but after meeting Wong Fei Hung and his men he was gradually convinced. One thing he knew with absolute certainty: there was no doubt that unlike Saddam Hussein's imaginary weapons of mass destruction, the United States could easily establish a link between Cuba and Angel Guzman.

If the existence of thermonuclear weapons in the drug lord's hands could be established, it could lead to a confrontation between Cuba that would make the missile crisis of October 1962 look like a school-yard scuffle, and might be just the excuse the Yankees wanted to invade his country.

So here he was, out of his element, literally about to take a leap into the darkness. There was a small buzzing from the headset in his ear. The pilot.

"*Lampara verde.*" Green light.

Cruz nodded to Wong. The grizzled Chinese veteran nodded back and turned to his men, barking a taut command.

"*Jiu zhu.*" Make ready.

Cruz and the others gripped the jump seats. There was a sudden yawning in the base of his stomach like an elevator dropping as the plane plunged several thousand feet. Suddenly his headset was filled with chatter from the pilot, who was talking to some invisible ground station, telling the controller that the flight had hit an air pocket. The chatter was drowned out by the droning of the hydraulic ramp mechanism as the rear door of the transport lowered, filling the aircraft with a howling backdraft.

"*Bao zhuang!*" Wong ordered. Packs on.

The five members of the team rose and began helping each other into the large, bulky packs, each one weighing slightly more than thirty kilos, almost seventy pounds. Cruz followed suit, shrugging into the complicated harness. Wong stepped in behind him as Cruz turned himself toward the lowering ramp. Faintly, over the roar of the wind, he heard the Velcro shearing behind him as the Chinese Special Forces leader opened the rear flaps.

This was where things wandered into the realm of insanity for Cruz. One of the five soldiers went to the forward cargo section and rolled back a circular aluminum tubing frame with a four-bladed propeller attached on a short spindle. Wong fitted the spindle over the small shaft jutting out from his backpack, locking the frame and propeller in. He then looped a control cable around Cruz's waist and strapped it to the Cuban's wrist. It had a single, one-button switch that fit under his thumb. That done, the Chinaman looped the two nylon control lines and their hand grips over Cruz's shoulders.

"Press the electronic start once you are airborne," instructed Wong for the hundredth time since he'd given Cruz the rushed training course. He spoke in Russian, the only language they shared. The ageless, flat Chinese face speaking with the distinctive slurring accent of a Muscovite was somehow a little disturbing. He sounded like the ghost of Arkady's father.

"To turn to the left pull on the left line, dump air, to turn to the right, pull on the right line, dump air. All very simple. To slow down, press the electronic start a second time and the engine will stop and you will begin to descend. Very simple. Engine can be stopped and started as many times as you wish during the flight. Easy as pie— you understand?"

"*Da*," Cruz answered, responding in his mother tongue. "*Ya vas ponimayu.*"

"Good," answered Wong. "Now we go."

Now the truly insane part of it all began. Cruz had never been claustrophobic; clearly someone who spent most of his time commanding a submarine could have no fear of small enclosed spaces. Nor was he an agoraphobe; the sea, after all, was an endless vista that often stretched to the horizon.

Being an birritumophobe, a person who has a deadly fear of nothingness, was something else again. "Mad" was the only word to describe someone willing to walk to the end of the Antonov's loading ramp and step off two miles above the surface of the earth into pitch blackness. Which, God help him, was exactly what he was about to do.

They didn't call them Flying Dragons for nothing. The squads had invented the concept of powered paraglider insertion into enemy territory. The equipment, based on an Italian technology and copied by the Chinese military engineers at the National Defense University in Beijing, added a lightweight twenty-two-horsepower engine and propeller unit to a paraglider.

With a direct-drive transmission and a sixteen-liter fuel cell, the entire unit weighed in at just under thirty kilograms and had a range of two hundred and ten miles over a period of six hours' flying time. This could be substantially increased by higher-altitude insertions and judicious hoarding of fuel by switching off the silenced engine for periods of the flight.

The insertions could be made with pinpoint accuracy and needed less than a hundred feet of open space to land. Of even more use, the paragliders, launched from the air, could just as easily be relaunched on foot from the ground.

The paragliders could cruise at heights of sixteen thousand feet to no more than a yard above the treetops.

The Antonov could easily explain its sudden drop in altitude as long as it maintained its course. The jungle target coordinates was barely a hundred miles, or three hours cruising speed time, from the drop, timed for a landing just at daybreak. Wong, carrying a GPS unit, his paraglider equipped with a shielded blue beacon light invisible from the ground, would lead the group in.

Eyes firmly shut, wind howling in his ears, and the ignition button under his thumb, Arkady pushed his way through the buffeting air, reached the lip of the loading ramp and stepped off, his scream of abject terror and the sudden adrenaline rush lost in the dark rush of air.

"*Chyort voz'mi!*" Arkady cursed and plunged into the bottomless belly of the night.

Finn Ryan stared into the dying coals of the small campfire and wondered if this time she'd bitten off more than she could chew. Garza and his bully boys were more than a simple escort for an archaeological survey team, that was certain. She wondered if, by some chance, the news had leaked about their discovery of the Codex Cortéz.

The four-hundred-year-old parchment had been a revelation and almost certainly the work of Hernán Cortéz himself, at least as transcribed into print by his Franciscan interpreter, Friar Gerónimo de Aguilar. The

Franciscan's tale was an astounding one, richly decorated with illustrations in the Mayan style.

According to the Codex, Cortéz worried that the great wealth in gold and gems that he had accumulated during the conquest of Mexico would be forfeited to the Queen of Spain on orders of Diego Velázquez de Cuéllar, the governor of Cuba and Cortéz's sworn enemy.

The excuse for the forfeiture would be that Cortéz had failed to deduct the *quinto*, or one-fifth of the wealth due to the crown, which in fact was quite true. If that didn't work, Cortéz knew that he would almost certainly be declared a heretic by the Inquisition, with which Velázquez de Cuéllar's family in Spain had close ties.

Not only would Cortéz be called back to Spain to stand before the Inquisitors, he would also likely be burned at the stake. The only way to avoid one or the other of these tragedies would be to make the entire, enormous hoard disappear.

With exactly that in mind, Cortéz gathered up his treasure and dispatched the Franciscan friar into the jungle with it, ordering him to hide the gold and gems until Cortéz's political future had been ensured. Friar Gerónimo was the perfect choice for the job; he'd been shipwrecked on the Yucatán coast years before, spoke the language fluently, and knew the customs.

According to the Codex, he also knew the perfect place to hide the golden hoard: an overgrown and forgotten temple deep in the jungle. Miraculously, the Codex gave vivid clues to the temple's location, and within a week or so of the discovery of the Codex, Finn and Billy were reasonably certain they knew where to look.

Unlike Cortéz, Finn and Billy were more than happy to share the benefits of their discovery with the government of Mexico, but the presence of "Dr." Garza and his men made her wonder if there wasn't something else going on. Garza's explanation that the team of heavily armed, hard-looking men who accompanied him were there to deal with *cocainistas* and rebels who might harm them was a little thin. Yucatán was a dangerous place all right, but the kind of jungle they were passing through didn't lend itself to the cultivation of opium poppies or the presence of any rebels she'd ever heard about.

Finn glanced at her wristwatch. Almost three thirty; if she didn't get back to sleep soon she was going to regret it. She looked beyond the fire. For soldiers supposedly protecting her, Eli, Guido, and Billy from harm, Garza's men weren't providing much in the way of sentry duty. A small area on the other side of the clearing they now occupied was set out with small nylon fly tents, and as far as Finn knew the entire six-man squad were tucked into their beds and sleeping.

She heard a faint rustling behind her in the jungle and turned quickly, her heart suddenly pounding in her chest, her night vision temporarily lost from staring into the small fire. She stood up, peering hard into the dappled interior of the forest. Once again she heard a small sound, closer now. She felt a soft touch on her shoulder and whirled, almost screaming.

"Some guard dog you'd make," her friend said and grinned. "Could have been a herd of elephants for all you'd care."

"There are no elephants in Mexico," said Finn. "And just what are you doing skulking around in the middle of the night?"

"It's not the middle of the night—it's early morning. And I wasn't skulking—I was snooping."

Billy squatted down beside the fire. Finn followed suit, keeping her voice low.

"Snooping where?"

"In the enemy camp," answered Billy.

"What enemy camp?" Finn asked.

"You know perfectly well who I'm talking about," snorted Billy. "You're just as suspicious of *El Doctoro Loco* over there as I am and don't deny it."

"Snooping for what?"

"Whatever I could find."

"And did you find anything?" Finn asked.

Billy reached into the pocket of his lightweight military-style shirt and handed her a strange object. It was plastic, had a clip on the back, and a two-inch-by-one-inch screen on the front.

According to the small label on the back, the item was manufactured by someplace called American Pacific Nuclear of Concord, California. Finn knew exactly what it was; she'd worn just such an item during her days as a postgraduate physical anthropology teaching assistant.

"Do you know what it is?" Billy asked.

"It's a thermoluminescent dosimeter," she answered. "A radiation detector."

"Every one of Garza's boys has one clipped to his pack."

"Why would they need something like that?" Finn asked.

"Same question I wanted an answer for," murmured her friend. Suddenly Billy yelped and stood up.

"What's wrong?"

Billy bent down and pulled up his pant leg. He grabbed something, crushing it between thumb and forefinger, and wrenched it off.

"Bugger!" said his lordship. "What the bloody hell is that?" He held the object up into the light of the fire. It looked like an immense wingless wasp, fully two inches long and a blackish red color. Its jaws were immense and there was a brutal-looking stinger on the end of its segmented body. Billy sagged to the ground, groaning. "My leg!"

"*Paraponera clavata!*" Finn said immediately. "A tropical bullet ant," she added, clearly frightened. She'd seen them years before, traveling with her parents, but never one as big as this. She crammed the radiation badge into her jeans and then whirled, dropping down and digging into her backpack.

"What are you looking for?" Billy groaned, clutching at his leg. His ankle had already begun to swell terribly and there was a line of heavy perspiration on his forehead. He had gone bone white.

"Benadryl!" Finn answered. "An antihistamine. It will take away some of the pain!"

"Hurry!" Billy moaned.

Then the screaming started. Hell had arrived on six legs.

19

Finn found the package of Benadryl, poked two capsules from the foil strip, and slid them under Billy's tongue. He was fully involved now, curled up into a fetal ball, shivering, his face coated in perspiration.

Quickly, Finn turned away, gathered up an armload of kindling from the pile and threw it onto the dying campfire. The flames roared up almost instantly, revealing the scene of horror all around them.

Garza's men came pouring from their tents. The sergeant, Mendez, stood in the flickering light of the flames, dressed only in his army-issue skivvies, his head tilted back, mouth wide open in a guttural roar of agonizing pain.

He was covered in an undulating cloak of the russet black insects. A sound could be heard beneath his rasping screams, a rustling like dried leaves in an autumn breeze, and there was a strange musky scent filling the air.

The enormous creatures twisted and curled, clawed mandibles biting into flesh as the stingers struck, pumping their deadly neurotoxin poisons deep beneath the skin.

Finn stared, petrified with horror, watching as streams of the huge, vicious ants swarmed and skittered up the sergeant's bare legs, disappearing beneath the loose boxers he was wearing.

As Finn watched, the soldier sank to his knees, and even more of the ants crawled up over his body as his hands flailed in front of his face in a vain effort to brush the never-ending horde of insects away. He tried to pull the creatures away from his mouth and eyes but failed, choking as they filled his throat and blinded him. Suffocating, he fell forward into a seething carpet of insects that was spread out around him in the jungle clearing, his voice abruptly stilled.

Two more of the soldiers appeared, stumbling out of their tents, screaming the way Mendez had. In seconds they were overwhelmed by the rolling, all-consuming terror coming from the jungle. The deadly insects were even coming down from the forest canopy.

There were tens of thousands of the creatures. They seemed to be moving in a steady phalanx across the clearing. Billy must have been bitten by one of the swarm's forward scouts.

Finn caught movement out of the corner of her eye as Eli came out of his pup tent, struggling into his hiking boots. Guido lurched out of his tent as well, staring across to the other side of the clearing beyond the fire.

"*Mierenneuker!*" whispered the bald-headed Dutchman.

Suddenly Garza appeared beside her, apparently unscathed by the attack. He had his backpack looped over one shoulder.

"Bullet ants," he said. "We must flee or be killed where we stand."

"What about your men?" Finn asked.

"My men are already dead. We are alive. We go."

"You can't just leave them!" Eli said, horrified by Garza's matter-of-fact tone. He glanced across the fire; Mendez was nothing more than an inhuman lump on the forest floor, his body invisible under the seething, undulating swarm of deadly ants.

"If you wish to be a hero you are welcome to rescue them. Make up your mind, young man. The creatures are almost upon us."

The Mexican was right. Another hundred feet and it would be too late for all of them.

"Guido, Eli, help me with Billy," ordered Finn, stooping down to her friend.

"Leave him," said Garza. "He will only slow us down."

"*Je kunt de pot op, aarsridder,*" replied Guido. With Eli he helped get a sagging, almost comatose Billy to his feet, then slung him over his shoulder in a fireman's lift. He turned to Finn. "Which way?"

"Doctor?" Finn asked.

"There," said Garza, barely hesitating, pointing to the northwest. "I can taste water in the air. A cenote. If we can reach it in time we may be safe."

"Go," said Finn, and with Garza in the lead and with one look behind, they went.

They found a trail through the forest almost immediately. It was narrow, almost to the point of nonexistence, probably made by some small mammals. The foliage on either side of the trail was a dense mixture of henequen, red ginger, and elephant ear, all ranged beneath the towering ceiba trees. As they raced down the path they could hear the screaming of the howler monkeys, disturbed by their frantic passage and the approaching legions of the deadly bullet ants.

Every few seconds Finn turned and looked back over her shoulder, but Guido seemed to be bearing Billy's weight without too much effort, the only sign of tension being the hard expression on the tall Dutchman's face. Ahead of her Garza ran on steadily, slashing at the encroaching foliage with his heavy-bladed *facao*, or machete.

Abruptly the jungle thinned and disappeared. In the darkness Finn could make out a crescent-shaped clearing, flat plates of limestone layered higher on one side of a large dark pool than the other.

Here and there a few mangroves clung to the stone, their open roots gnarled as the tendons of a corpse. On the far side of the cenote the foliage was much denser, bean bushes and hibiscus cascading over the edge in lush waterfalls.

They stepped out onto the stone slabs around the low end of the pool. The cenote was no more than thirty feet across, about twice the size of a backyard swimming pool. Guido gently lowered Billy to the ground. He seemed a little better but he was still woozy.

"Can you walk?" Finn asked.

Billy shook his head. "Don't think so," he slurred. "Just need a minute or two."

"We don't have a minute or two," said Garza bluntly. "I estimate that the swarm is at least a hundred meters wide and God only knows how deep. The average speed of an army ant swarm is eleven-point-six kilometers an hour. I estimate these creatures are making almost twice that. They will be here in a matter of seconds now."

"What do we do?" Finn asked.

In answer Garza swung the backpack down from his shoulder and took out a large bottle of some clear liquid.

"Tequila?" Eli said, astounded.

"Close," said Garza, grimacing. "Isopropyl alcohol. Drench your feet and ankles in it. Douse your clothes thoroughly. Señor Derlagen," Garza ordered, turning to the Dutchman, "I'm afraid you'll have to lift his lordship off the ground when they come."

"Why rubbing alcohol?" Guido asked.

"It's fatal to ants of all species," answered Garza, unscrewing the bottle cap and pouring the fluid onto his boots and legs. He handed the bottle to Finn. "Now you." She did as she was told, then passed the bottle on. There was a rustling sound from behind her and a dark musty scent filled her nostrils, so acrid she wanted to cough.

"They're close," Finn said.

"What do we do if the alcohol doesn't work?" Eli asked. "Jump into the pool?"

"No good," said Garza. "There's a whole class of workers whose job it is to smooth the path for the others. Pothole fillers. They'll cover the surface of the cenote and let their brethren walk over them to the other side. Then they'll drown. Legionary behavior. Anything for the greater good even if it means death."

"The Borg," said Eli.

"I have never heard of this Borg," answered Garza.

"Why am I not surprised?"

"They are here," said Guido, staring back into the forest. He bent and picked up Billy again, hoisting him over his shoulder.

The ants came like a viscous flow of lava, oozing out of the forest with the strange chitinous rustling of ten million legs brushing against each other, the air filling with the pungent odor of formic acid vapor, the ant version of a battle cry.

They poured forward blindly but in perfect formation, three hundred feet across, climbing over small obstructions and each other, continuing in a terrible march. They pushed past everything before them, including skittering hordes of beetles, centipedes, cockroaches, and millions of spiders, all-fleeing from the all-engulfing army of two-inch sting monsters in their russet body armor, like the ancient Roman legions whose behavior the creatures mimicked eerily.

"They're all gigantic," whispered Finn, staring into the darkness. She put her arm up over her mouth and nose to stifle the overwhelming chemical stench as her eyes began to water. "This isn't right."

"They're mutants, culled through more than four hundred generations."

"You seem to know a whole hell of a lot about ants, my friend," said Eli. "Especially these ants."

"Be still," ordered Garza. "They are upon us."

And all around them, as well, rolling forward inexorably, even pouring into the water to make enormous crustlike rafts of themselves on the still water of the cenote, allowing their fiendish legions of companions to get to the other side.

Within less than a minute they were completely surrounded by the swarm, protected by the small zone of alcohol spread on their clothes and sprinkled on the bare limestone around them.

The formic acid vapors became almost suffocating, their throats stinging with it and their eyes streaming with tears. The horde seemed never-ending, but after almost ten minutes the numbers began to thin and then, miraculously, they were gone and the forest became silent, empty of the smallest cry, whatever creatures that had survived stunned into silence by the terrible passage of the immense marauding swarm.

"Okay," said Finn, unable to hold back the fury in her tone. "Enough of this. Tell us just what's going on here, Garza. And don't try to feed me any crap about being an archaeologist. Just who the hell are you?"

20

The sun was rising, bringing hot mists rising from the jungle's humid floor and sending blinding stabs of light through the heavy canopy of ceiba trees and thatch palms. Eli and Guido had ventured back to the old camp to see what could be salvaged.

A bed of palm fronds and huge lurid green leaves from the elephant ear plants that grew beside the cenote had been made by Finn and Garza for Billy, who seemed to be sleeping comfortably now, the swelling in his lower leg gradually subsiding. They'd built another fire, this one well out on the limestone shelf.

The surface of the water was still clogged with huge floating masses of the dead bullet ants sacrificed for the common good of the swarm. The air was still filled with the formic acid stink of their passage, but the smell seemed to be keeping the mosquitoes and other bugs away, which was a relief.

A green jay, which was actually bright yellow except for its black-feathered head and neck, scolded them from the twisted branches of a calabash tree, and a tyrant flycatcher made a reconnaissance pass over the cenote and the masses of drowned, half-submerged ants that floated on the surface. Somewhere in the forest a mot-mot bird let out its croaking, far-reaching call. Every now and again the surface of the water splashed as curious fish tasted the free breakfast above them.

"Is your name even Garza?"

"Yes, Ruben Filiberto Garza."

"But you're not an archaeologist."

"No. I am an operations officer with CISEN, the Centro de Investigación y Seguridad Nacional, the Center for Research on National Security. Like your own Central Intelligence Agency."

"Well, that makes me feel a whole lot better." Finn grimaced. "How come you know so much about ants? Doesn't seem like much of a subject for study by a spy. And what does it have to do with me?" She glanced over at Billy on his makeshift bed of greenery. He seemed to be stirring.

"Almost ten years ago an entomologist named Esteban Ruiz from the Universidad Nacional Autónoma de México campus in Merida noticed an upswing in mutations among several species that seemed to be concentrated in the Yucatán Peninsula."

"Not just ants?"

"No. Spiders, mosquitoes, several kinds of beetle. Many. The same thing had been noted in the cenotes, except it was not insects, it was fish and small crustaceans. And there was degradation of some fungi and bacteria as well. It was very perturbing because it seemed to have no source."

"Ten years ago?"

"Yes."

"And nothing was done about it?"

"In Mexico it sometimes takes a great deal of time for these things to rise to people's attention."

"Not just Mexico," said Finn. The Internet had been invented in 1973 by a computer scientist named Vinton Cerf and an engineer named Robert Kahn, but no one really paid attention for the better part of twenty years. Einstein figured out the famous $E=MC^2$ equation in 1905 but it took another forty years to invent the atom bomb. "What happened?"

"At first the mutations were seen as singularities, perhaps caused by sunspots or the degradation of the ozone layer."

"But?"

"The mutations persisted. Not only that, they seemed to regularize, useful mutations weeding out the bad. This seemed to point to a large, central point of origination."

"Two-inch bullet ants," said Finn.

"And their massive colony size. Prior to these mutations the ants were local foragers with very little social organization; now as you have seen they've developed the mass hunting traits of army ants."

"Could it have been some kind of inbreeding between the species?"

"They say at the university that such a thing is possible but very unlikely."

"And this is the reason your men were all wearing radiation badges?"

"You knew?"

"Billy was curious." Finn turned to her friend again, then turned back to Garza. "His curiosity may have been what got him bitten. He was on your side of the camp just before."

"Too bad."

"What exactly were you doing up at that time of the night?"

"Satisfying my own curiosity. It seemed far too much of a coincidence that your destination was so close to what we consider the center of the mutation effect. Ground Zero, if you will."

"We told the government officials the exact truth, Dr. Garza…"

"Colonel, actually."

"Colonel Garza then. We didn't try to pull the wool over anybody's eyes. We discovered a copy of an ancient Codex that indicates, mostly by way of astral navigation as the Mayan people knew it, that there was a hidden temple close to the GPS point we indicated.

"We checked with remote-sensing arrays and with the geophysical people at both my own university in Ohio and with the people at NASA. According to available satellite data there are a number of anomalies in the area— remains of old roadways and trails, thin spots in vegetation, regular shapes including one that might be a temple site, all of which add up to the probability that there's something man-made out there in the jungle."

Garza turned away for a minute and began digging around in his knapsack. Behind her Billy was sitting up.

"Wha' hap'ned?" he asked froggily. He cleared his throat and tried again. "What happened?"

"You were bitten by an ant."

"One ant?"

"Just one."

"Good Lord!"

"You were lucky. The one that bit you had a few million friends."

"Miss Ryan?"

Finn turned back to Garza. "Yes?"

The colonel handed her a stiff piece of photographic paper. There was a multicolored image on it with one glowing yellow spot in the center, a vague oblong.

"It may surprise you to know that Mexico operates its own satellite fleet. This is a blowup of the sector in question taken by Satmex Seven. The satellite was only launched three months ago, which is why we didn't notice it before."

Finn saw from the coordinates that the oblong glow was within a thousand yards of her objective, perhaps even closer.

"What is it?"

"A radiographic satellite image of the GPS coordinates you gave to the museum people."

"What's the hot spot?"

"Plutonium-239, very small traces."

"Could it be natural?"

"Plutonium-239 does not exist in nature."

"Which means that what you see in that photograph is man-made."

"Bloody hell!" Billy murmured, getting weakly to his feet. "A bomb?"

"Indeed so, Your Lordship. A hydrogen bomb."

"Crikey!" Billy whispered. He staggered forward and looked at the picture over Finn's shoulder.

"That's impossible," said Finn.

"I'm afraid it's quite possible," said Garza.

"Explain."

"On Monday, December 24, 1962, in the early-morning hours a B-47 bomber was flying reconnaissance patterns on the edge of Cuban airspace. This was only two months after the Cuban missile crisis, you must remember. No one remembers it today, but there was a large tropical storm front over the Yucatán that night."

"The aircraft went down?" Finn asked.

"Presumably into the gulf. Our American friends didn't see fit to tell their allies to the south about it."

"The plane was carrying nuclear weapons?" Billy asked.

"Yes. Two B-43 MOD-1 hydrogen bombs."

"Our government didn't ask for Mexico's help?" asked Finn.

"Relations were somewhat strained back then. As now, Mexico supported the United States in matters of foreign policy but at the same time refused to break off diplomatic relations with Castro. We weren't to be trusted, certainly not with information like that."

"So the U.S. government chose to assume that the plane crashed into the sea?" Billy asked.

"It would seem so. They probably sent a few U-2 flights over the area but clearly they found nothing." He shrugged. "The jungle is very jealous of her secrets. She does not give them up easily."

"So why not simply inform them now?" Finn asked.

"Relations are not much better today than they were in 1962. All this talk of illegal immigrants, drugs. It would be a terrible embarrassment to both countries. The United States interfering with Mexico, Mexico keeping vital information from America. There is also another possibility." Garza paused. "A much more dangerous one."

"Such as?" Finn said.

"We are well aware that Cuba has been trading with the drug cartels for a very long time. Drugs are a source of hard currency for them. Revolutions cost money and they can't be paid for in bananas or sugarcane. What if the Soviet Union had brought atomic warheads into Cuba in 1962 and simply removed them to the Yucatán for safekeeping while Kennedy and Khrushchev argued? If such warheads were discovered and were found to be of Soviet origin, it would be a disaster. It might even provide the stimulus for an American invasion of Cuba.

"Kennedy promised that would never happen, didn't he? Publicly?" Billy interrupted.

Garza smiled coldly. "He did. He was also assassinated within a year. Kennedy is long dead. The present administration does not feel bound to honor promises made more than forty years ago. They seem not to honor promises made five minutes ago. It is a pragmatic age we live in. Money is power. We would very much like not to be put in the middle of this problem."

"So what do you intend to do?" Finn asked.

"Find them, dispose of them. If there are no bombs there is no problem."

"What's to stop you?"

"A man named Angel Guzman."

21

Angel Guzman sat behind the desk in the headquarters building of his jungle camp smoking a cigar and listening to the rattle of rain on the tin roof over his head. The plump little madman sipped brandy from his personal Starbucks coffee mug and eyed the young, handsome figure of Harrison Noble tied to the plain kitchen chair next to the woodstove. The stove had been banked with kindling and the surface of the cast iron was steaming as errant drops of rain leaking from the roof hissed and danced on the hot metal. Harrison Noble was naked. There were circular boils on most areas of his exposed skin where Angel Guzman had applied the hot tip of his cigar.

Harrison Noble had been crying. He had also been screaming for most of the night. It was early morning now. Angel Guzman wasn't trying to extract information from the young man; he knew everything worth knowing. He was simply torturing him as an exercise in power. It was the kind of thing his people expected of him. He was known for inflicting unceasing pain on anyone who became his enemy. Angel Guzman was not the most astute politician in the world, but he knew that power not exercised was not power at all and could very well be considered its opposite: weakness.

Like most megalomaniac psychotics, Angel Guzman was not a man who saw his life as a sequence of well-ordered events based on a series of logical steps, but rather as a series of brilliantly clear images of himself in various situations.

As a child he'd regularly seen himself as Christ, sitting astride a donkey, glowing faintly as he rode through his village, just like the brightly colored picture in his Sunday school book. This had nothing at all to do with the other things the priest had him do in the little church vestry after mass, but the image remained: he was the savior of his village. Other images included riding in a limousine up to the Imperial Palace in Mexico City in the uniform of a general, pictures of himself with various movie stars, sipping champagne on a private jet, and one, a special favorite, of himself greeting the Pope and the Pope kissing his ring rather than the other way around. Right now, watching Harrison Noble squirming in the kitchen chair on the other sides of the room, Guzman was seeing himself in the Oval Office of the White House enjoying a photo opportunity with the president. It seemed very realistic.

"Why is it," said the man with the little pot-belly, "that Americans think they are smarter than anyone they perceive as speaking with an accent?"

"What?" the younger Noble asked numbly.

"Your president cannot pronounce the name of the country he has invaded, but he thinks Mexicans are lesser beings because they do not speak English well. You are very arrogant, you Americans. There were people speaking Spanish when your ancestors were living in thatch-roofed huts on the coast of Ireland."

"Don't understand," muttered Harrison Noble.

"No, of course you don't. You thought you and your hired thugs could come into my jungle, steal what you wanted and perhaps kill me in the process, isn't that right."

"This wasn't what we agreed," said Noble.

"No," said Guzman, smiling.

"You broke your word."

"What did you expect?" Guzman laughed. "After all, I am nothing but a peasant living in the jungle, not an honorable upstanding man like James Jonas Noble."

"We had a deal."

"So we did. Your father's company wanted the rights to any pharmaceutical plants it discovered in the sector of the Yucatán that I control. In return I was to get a portion of the profits. An equitable arrangement. On the surface."

"You agreed," croaked Harrison Noble.

"I wasn't aware at the time that you already knew what you were looking for, nor how valuable it was. You told me Noble Pharmaceuticals was looking for an over-the-counter medication for constipation. Another one of America's endless elixirs to move their bowels. What is this new drug your father wishes to bring to market next year?"

"Celatropamine."

"A drug that allows you to eat as much as you want and still lose weight, correct?"

"Yes."

"A gold mine. Better than Viagra."

"Yes."

"And?"

"With the extract from your plant it becomes incredibly addictive."

"So the gold mine becomes a diamond mine."

"Yes."

"But you didn't tell me this. You also did not tell me that the same additive to my cocaine does the same thing, increases its addictiveness a thousand times. You wanted to keep it all to yourselves."

"You know there is a limited supply until we synthesize it. There are only the plants close to the temple."

"The ones that have grown through many generations, mutating on top of my hydrogen bombs."

"We don't care about the bombs. Just the plants."

"So you come to steal them." Guzman sighed. He got up from his desk and went out onto the wide veranda of the headquarters building.

"Fetch the prisoner," he ordered the guard on duty. The man disappeared into the tin-roofed hut and dragged out Harrison Noble, still naked and tied to his chair.

In the sodden courtyard puddles had formed in the mud at the base of a T-shaped scaffold that had been hammered deeply into the soil. A man hung upside down from each jutting arm of the scaffold.

Two of the Blackhawk soldiers had been picked off in the initial ambush, but Tibor Cherka, the leader, and his second in command, a man named Bostick, had managed to survive. Like Harrison Noble they had been stripped of their clothes. They had been hanging upside down in the rain all night. Their hands were chained together and their heads hung a foot or so from the mud.

The rain fell in steady lines down the slanted veranda roof with a continuous sloshing sound. The two Black-hawk men were far beyond making any noise at all, although both were fully conscious.

"So foolish," said Angel Guzman. "Thinking that you could get away with it using only four men. Now you have left me with this mess to deal with."

"We just wanted the plants," moaned Harrison Noble, staring at the two soaking men on the scaffolds.

"To think that the simple yellow allamanda would prove so valuable. *Allamanda cathartica*. It grows like a weed in Mexico, and it will make me rich."

"You won't be able to synthesize it yourself. You need us to refine it."

"I think our Cuban friends could do the job quite well. Imagine what access to this celatropamine drug could do to their economy."

"You made a deal with my father!"

"You made a deal with the devil," answered Guzman.

The fat little drug lord with the thinning hair walked over to where the guard was standing beside Harrison Noble's chair and slid the machete out of the man's green canvas sheath. The machete was nothing special. It was stained, nicked, and its handle wrapped with black tape. It was two feet long and very sharp.

Without another word or any sort of hesitation, Angel Guzman hefted the machete in his hand, walked down the veranda steps, and crossed the courtyard in the rain. He stopped in front of the T-shaped scaffold and swept the blade around sharply, striking at Tibor Cherka's exposed waistline with a practiced back-hand like a tennis player. The first strike sliced through flesh to the spine. The second cut took out the spine itself and continued deeper. The third cut, this one a forehand from the opposite side, completely severed Cherka's torso from the rest of his dangling body.

The torso, still obviously alive, writhed in the mud, Cherka's mouth opening and closing but making no sound. His organs spilled out as he twisted and turned, eyes bulging.

Harrison Noble, although he hadn't eaten in some time, vomited into his lap.

Ignoring the thing twisting in the mud, Guzman climbed back up the veranda steps, rinsed the machete off in the overflow from the tin roof, and slid the weapon back into the guard's sheath. The guard showed no particular expression. Guzman crossed to Harrison Noble and patted him lightly on the shoulder.

"We have done experiments. Hung that way for so long, all the blood rushes to the brain. He will live for six or seven minutes, the brain fully functional, trying to figure some way out of his predicament. It can be quite amusing."

"You're mad!"

"That's the least of your problems, Mr. Noble, I assure you. You're going to have to explain to Daddy why you failed."

"You're letting me go?"

"In a while. After I've had a little more fun at your expense. And when I do I'm even going to send a sample back with you. The plants of course have been moved by now, as have the bombs themselves, but I'm sure your father and I can come to some arrangement."

Cherka's torso had slithered closer to the veranda, leaving a greasy trail of entrails behind.

"I think he wants to talk to you," said Guzman. "Shall I give him a hand up the steps?"

Harrison Noble threw up again.

22

Lord William Pilgrim lay prone in the tall grass at the edge of the jungle clearing and watched silently, holding back a scream of very unlordlylike terror as a gooey reddish white stream of inch-long worms slithered over the back of his hand and headed south, roughly in the direction of his belt line.

"I'm going to scream if you don't mind," he said. "I've had just about enough of this insect stuff."

Garza swept up a handful of the rust-colored creatures and popped them into his mouth. He chewed happily and swallowed.

"Dear God!" Billy whispered, appalled. Finn, lying beside him on the other side, plucked one of the worms off his wrist and sucked it between her lips.

Billy gagged.

"Maguey worms. Caterpillars, actually," explained Finn, smiling. "They're the worms you find in the bottom of bottles of Mescal."

"Much better fried in butter with a little garlic," added Garza. "Lots of protein as well."

"*Jij eet smegmakaas!*" muttered Guido, who'd watched the whole procedure, eyes wide.

"You're both wussies," Finn said and grinned.

"Can anyone explain why we're all lying here in the bushes eating bugs and whispering?" Eli Santoro asked. He reached under his eye patch with his index finger and scratched.

"Because we're being careful," answered Garza, the Mexican spy. He squirmed a little, dug into the backpack beside him and took out a very sophisticated pair of Steiner military binoculars. He scanned the clearing for a long moment and then handed the compact device to Finn. She stared through the ultra-clear lenses, concentrating on what at first glance appeared to be a low hill at the far side of the jungle clearing. The hill was four-sided with a tall, almost chimney-like protrusion just off center. It was covered in undergrowth and was topped by several tall, spreading acacia trees, their thick roots like claws digging into the jungle soil with dark, gnarled fingers.

"A temple perhaps?" Garza said quietly.

"Too small," murmured Finn, scanning the shape. "Less than fifty feet square."

"A natural formation?" Billy asked.

"The jungle here is flat as a tortilla," said Finn. "Yucatán is basically a single limestone plateau. Anything sticking up like that is sticking up for a reason."

"A sacrificial altar," Eli Santoro said.

"You've been watching too many Mel Gibson movies," Garza said. "The Mayans didn't spend every last minute cutting people's hearts out. They had an empire to run, among other things. Commerce. Trade. Agriculture. A whole military subculture."

"Science," said Finn quietly, focusing the binoculars on the dark scar in the soil directly in front of the mound. "It's a miniature *coyocan*."

"What is this *coyocan*?" Guido asked, flicking one of the maguey caterpillars off his wrist with a faint shudder.

"It's the Mayan word for snail," explained Finn. "That thing's like a chimney. Get close enough and I'll bet you'll find what's left of a spiral staircase inside that tower. An observatory. There's a massive one at Chichen Itza."

"Why have such a thing here?" Garza asked.

"I don't know," said Finn. "And why is it so small? As though they were trying to keep it hidden. A secret."

"Maybe that's exactly what they intended," answered Garza.

"What about your bombs?" Finn asked, handing Garza the binoculars.

"Gone," answered the Mexican. "You can see where the excavation was."

"Inside the temple thing?" Billy asked.

"Doubtful," said Garza, peering through the glasses again. "There's a trail off on the right. It looks as though they were dug up and then dragged off somewhere to the north."

"All right," said Billy. "You've seen where your bombs have gone, we've surveyed the temple thingee, and I'm being eaten by mosquitoes and every other kind of nasty creature your wretched Yucatán Peninsula has to offer. Can we consider the survey done and beat a hasty retreat?" The Englishman sighed. "What I wouldn't give for a pint of Thwaites Best Mild right now."

"We're not going anywhere just yet," said Garza. "We're talking about World War Three, not a couple of firecrackers."

"And I want to know why there's a Mayan observatory in the middle of nowhere," said Finn.

"Everywhere around here is the middle of nowhere," grumbled Billy.

Garza continued to scan the clearing with the binoculars. Finally he put them down and turned to Finn. "In some ways I agree with his lordship," said the Mexican. "Guzman and his men must be nearby. To remain here is foolish bravado. I could be back here in force within four or five days. It would be safer if you and your friends were not here at all."

"This man Guzman has already moved your bombs once. He could do it again," responded Finn. "You said there was a chance the Cubans were involved. Could they get the bombs to the coast? Get them to Cuba?"

"There are rumors…" said Garza hesitantly.

"Rumors?"

"Foolishness. There is talk of a phantom submarine that Guzman uses to transport his narcotics."

"A Cuban submarine?" Eli Santoro scoffed. "They don't have enough gasoline to put in the limo Ted Turner gave him a few years back, let alone a submarine. That's crazy talk."

"The Cubans have some close friends in Venezuela. Sympathetic ones. Don't let your patriotism blind you to reality. If Fidel wants to keep a submarine in play, he has the means to do so. The idea is one my office takes quite seriously."

"So they could get the bombs out of Yucatán?"

"It's possible."

"You must have had a plan," said Finn. "You had some idea of what you were going to do. You can't tell me you came in blind."

"Yes."

"So what was the plan?"

"Disable the bombs. Destroy the plutonium cores if necessary."

"Disable as in explode?"

"Remove the cores, explode the mechanisms. One thing we know for sure, the Cubans have no nuclear program."

"But they could trade the plutonium."

"Yes."

"Can you do it by yourself, without your men?" Billy asked.

"With some help. Someone who knows a little of electronics."

"That would be me," said Eli.

"Some physical strength."

"Hello there," said the big bald Dutchman. "*Ik heet Guido Derlagen.*"

"This is Mexico's problem. I cannot have you involved," said Garza, shaking his head.

"What about the necessary explosives?"

"In the pack," said Garza. "Two shaped charges."

"And radiation?" Billy asked. "You weren't wearing those badges for nothing."

"It is not really a problem, at least in the short term," Garza explained. "The cores in the bombs are covered in hexagonal plates of explosive. Plutonium can be obtained from special-purpose plutonium production reactors, or as a by-product of commercial power or research reactors. The plutonium produced by special-purpose production reactors has a relatively low plutonium-240 content, less than seven percent, and is called weapons grade. Commercial reactors may produce plutonium with Pu-240 with concentrations of more than twenty percent and is called reactor grade, but because it must be handled remotely it is not economic to make bombs with.

Weapons grade really means cheap. A pair of rubber gloves would be good enough. The cores only need to be separated from the shaped charges. Sinking them in a cenote would be good enough for the time being."

"How about the observatory over there?" Finn suggested.

"What do you mean?" Garza asked.

"I'll bet that structure is seated directly over a cenote pool," said Finn. "It's often how Mayan and Aztec astronomers worked. They used a cenote pool or an artificial disk of still water to reflect the night sky for easier study. They even had numbered grids in some of them with painted lines or rows of stones as dividers to map the entire sky."

"What are you suggesting?" Garza asked.

"You, Guido, and Eli see if you can track down the bombs. Billy and I will find the entrance to the temple. I can almost guarantee a cenote for your plutonium. We drop the cores in the pool. The perfect hiding place, at least for a little while. Until you can call in the cavalry." She turned and glanced at Eli and Guido. "Did you find any tools back at the campsite?"

"Couple of folding shovels, mountaineering axes. Some rope, trowels. A few flares. Basic stuff. Nothing fancy."

"It should be enough. There won't be much blocking the entrance. It doesn't look like the structure's been over-built very much, if at all. Virgin territory."

"Then what?" Billy asked, lying between Garza and Finn. "A game of whist perhaps?"

"We run like hell," said Finn.

23

Cardinal Rossi, dressed in a natty pair of Greg Norman single-pleat golf shorts, a dark blue Ben Hogan golf shirt, and a top-of-the-line pair of FootJoy shoes, addressed the ball carefully and whacked the little white orb two hundred yards down the fifth fairway of the Windsor Downs Golf Course on Cat Cay. He watched its flight, tilting his head slightly as the ball arced over the expansive sod and headed toward the green. Not bad for an old man with a bit of bursitis.

"Looks like God's on your side," James Noble said, grumbling as the ball dropped straight as a die.

"Always." Rossi smiled. "One of the perks of the job." He dropped his titanium driver into his golf bag and began pulling the cart down the fairway. "Heard from your son lately?"

"He's been out of contact for the last few days."

"He's in the jungle?"

"Yes."

"With your friends?"

"Yes."

"I'm worried," said the cardinal.

"There's no reason for you to worry about anything."

"There's always a reason to worry about everything," answered the cardinal. "I've been at the Vatican for the better part of half a century. I've seen everything from murders to miracles. Worry accompanies both and everything in between. Control is everything."

"I've got it under control," Noble said. His relationship with the Italian was a continuing source of irritation. How could you expect a man who believed in virgin births to know anything about business?

"No, you don't," said the cardinal flatly. "You've involved the Church with a Mexican drug lord and a Cuban dictator."

"Not the Church," argued Noble. "One of the banks owned by the Church."

"Don't be an idiot. The relationship leads right back to the Vatican."

"You mean to the Twelve," said Noble.

"Don't try to threaten me with what you think you know, Mr. Noble. Last year your company did twelve billion dollars in business. Of that twelve billion roughly half was invested on your behalf by friends of mine. Powerful friends."

"Now who's doing the threatening?" Noble snorted.

"I never threaten, Mr. Noble. I merely inform."

"What are you saying?"

"If Noble Pharmaceuticals doesn't get celatropamine to the marketplace within the next eighteen months your losses are going to be immense. If there is any chance of that happening, Banco Venizia will withdraw its support immediately."

"Why? Drugs take time to introduce. It's not as though we need FDA approval. Celatropamine is an additive, not a drug in its own right."

They reached the spot on the fairway that held the cardinal's ball. He chose a smaller Callaway wood, barely hesitated, and knocked the ball easily up onto the green.

"I am a prudent man, Mr. Noble. I research things. Celatropamine is listed as a nutrient additive with the Federal Drug Administration in the United States. When the FDA discovers that celatropamine enhances the addictive potential of anything it is combined with from toothpaste to baby formula, there is going to be an immediate attempt by your government to have the drug restricted if not banned outright. Celatropamine added to cigarettes, for instance. Good God, man!"

"I thought that was your interest in the first place," said Noble as they tromped toward the patch of brighter green in the middle distance.

"Which brings us back to the question of control. Too many people are becoming involved. A leak would be disastrous."

"There won't be any leak," Noble said. "My son has been given strict instructions."

"Regarding Guzman?"

"Yes."

"The Cubans?"

"Yes."

"You have the assets necessary to deal with the situation?"

"The best."

"When will you know?"

"Tomorrow night. That's when the extraction is to take place."

"He'll have the necessary sample?"

"If he doesn't I'll kill him," said Noble.

Rossi reached his ball and took a lovely new Ping putter out of the bag. He knelt with the putter and lined up the shot. It was twenty-five feet uphill with a slight break to the right. He tossed a grass clipping into the air. Barely any breeze. The cardinal stood, took a deep breath, and let it out slowly. He turned to Noble, his expression blank.

"If he doesn't, I'll kill you," he said. He turned back to the ball and made the putt.

Max Kessler stood in the middle of Boulder Bridge in Rock Creek Park, his hands clasped together as he stared over the edge at the shallow waters of the little stream that ran beneath the old single span built back before the twenties. Except for the faint burbling of the water below and the sighing of the breeze in the trees all around, there was only silence. There hadn't been a vehicle on the road behind him for the better part of half an hour now. It was a nice evening, the last light of a summer day in Washington, D.C., fading gracefully away into night. The trees were heavy enough to prevent the use of line-of-sight optical lasers to record voices and the tumbling waters directly below the bridge would make any wiring of his companion useless if he was being set up for some sort of sting operation. Kessler also had a vibrating pocket detector in his suit jacket that would pick up virtually any RF signal from a transmitter, just in case.

The very tall bald-headed man standing beside him was Dr. Simon Andrew Grunnard. Grunnard wore heavy horn-rim spectacles and orthopedic shoes. He was a senior research scientist for Noble Pharmaceuticals and director of their ethno-botanical research division. He had come to Max Kessler through a long and careful chain of connections that originated in Las Vegas and meandered across the nation to the Noble Research Center in Chapel Hill, North Carolina.

"Perhaps we should begin," murmured Kessler.

"I'm not sure if I'm doing the right thing," answered Grunnard.

"I'm not your conscience, Doctor. I am here to facilitate your interests and further my own. I am not here to discuss right and wrong with you."

"This is hard for me."

"That's too bad," said Kessler. "And frankly, sir, I don't really care. What do you know about celatropamine?"

"Noble Pharmaceuticals is about to release a form of the drug trade-named Celedawn."

"A weight-loss remedy."

"Yes."

"In what form?"

"An over-the-counter nutrient bar."

"A meal replacement?"

"Yes."

"When?"

"Eight months. We're waiting for a sample of the base nutrient to be delivered."

"What is a base nutrient?"

"A plant extract from which the drug can be synthesized."

"The drug can't be synthesized without it?"

"Eventually, but it's much easier to clone molecules from the original plant source. It's why they send ethnobotanist plant hunters to the Amazon."

"You discovered celatropamine?"

"The original plant base, yes. In the Yucatán."

"As I understand it the drug comes from some sort of mutated plant."

"Yes, a small concentration of radically altered *Allamanda cathartica*. I've never seen it anywhere else."

"You brought some back to Chapel Hill?"

"Yes. Enough for small-scale studies."

"But not for synthesis."

"No."

"The drug is apparently highly addictive, yes?"

"Not the drug itself. It makes whatever it's added to addictive to an incredible degree."

"So people will become addicted to these Celedawn bars then."

"Yes. The bars are already a laxative. Someone on a diet of nothing but the bars will lose weight very swiftly. The long-term effects could be quite dangerous, however. Dehydration, for one."

"Celatropamine can be added to other products?"

"Yes."

"With the same result?"

"Yes."

"And if news of the drug was released prematurely?"

"It would probably be banned almost immediately."

"Causing great losses to Noble Pharmaceuticals."

"Yes."

"Or great wealth if you knew beforehand the drug was going to be banned before it ever reached the market. You could sell the stocks short."

"I don't know anything about stock trading, but as I understand it, yes."

"And you have stock options?"

"I've worked at Noble for twenty-five years. Right from the start."

"And now you wish to retire a wealthy man."

"I suppose that's a blunt way of putting it," said Grunnard.

"I am a blunt man, Doctor."

"Can you help me?" asked the ethno-botanist.

"We can help each other." Max Kessler smiled. He put his hand under the taller man's elbow and guided him across the bridge. "Let's walk a little and discuss details."

24

They smelled the camp before they saw it.

The rank odor of a hundred or so men living in close quarters and rarely bathing. Body odor, human waste, and the sweet-sour smell of food cooking over charcoal fires. By the time they reached the edge of the large clearing it was almost sunset, the guard towers standing out in stark silhouette against the dying sun.

"How do we get in?" Eli Santoro asked in a whisper. Beside him, prone in the last of the foliage at the jungle's edge, Garza peered through his binoculars. The camp was a huge rectangle with a wall of bulldozed dirt topped by a palisade of bamboo stakes. There were two guards in each of the towers manning .50-caliber machine guns. There was a large front gate made of bamboo and barbed wire with four more guards. Over the top of the bamboo palisade they could see the crumbled ruins of an old temple at the far end of the camp. There was a surprising amount of noise—shouting voices, laughter, and a general growling undertone of sound.

"Noisy," commented Guido, who was carrying Garza's pack across his broad shoulders. He passed one hand over his big bald head in a nervous gesture.

"Careless," answered Garza. "They don't care who hears them."

"They're in the middle of the jungle, why should they care?" scoffed Eli.

"Because of people like us," said Garza grimly.

"You still haven't answered my question," said Eli. "How do we get past the guards and the towers?"

"The ruins," answered Garza. "It's the only blind spot from the towers."

Like most ancient Mayan temples, the one that formed part of the eastern wall of the camp had been built in stages over a number of centuries, each dynasty adding on to the one that had gone before. This particular one, never discovered, excavated, or looted, was at least twenty-five hundred years old and at one time must have loomed at least a hundred feet above the jungle floor. Now it stood barely twenty feet above the ground and was covered with vines, trees, and dense foliage, barely recognizable as man-made.

It took Garza, Eli, and Guido the better part of half an hour to move around to the far end of the clearing, and by then the shadows had deepened even further. Garza was right; where the temple wall rose over the wall of bermed earth there was no palisade and the wall itself was angled slightly, just enough to make it impossible to see from either of the corner guard towers. The trio waited another fifteen minutes until full dusk and then simply walked into the clearing and quickly clambered up through the maze of vines and foliage that covered the slightly sloping pyramid wall.

"Now what?" Eli said as they settled down behind the decayed remains of what had once been a huge stone statue of a jaguar set at the corner of the wall. The long rectangular compound was spread out below them. There was a large main building with a tin roof and set on stilts to the north, a number of smaller barracks buildings against the south wall by the main gate, and a large, World War II–style Quonset hut at the opposite end of the compound. In front of the Quonset hut an open–fly tent had been set up on metal poles. Beneath the open canvas several bright arc lights had been set up, thick rubber cables running back to the hut. They could hear the muffled sound of a thumping generator coming from inside the Quonset hut. The two bombs had been set out on heavy wooden trestles that looked as though they had been specially constructed for the job. There were four men under the canvas cover, three of them apparently disassembling the devices, the fourth man supervising. All four men were dressed in military uniform, unlike the pattern of the camouflage worn by the guards and other personnel they could see within the compound. All four were wearing surgical masks and all four were Chinese.

"*Oosters?*" Guido queried.

"What the hell are the Chinese doing here?" Eli said.

There was the distinctive sound of an automatic pistol being cocked.

"Perhaps I could ask you the same question," said an accented voice out of the darkness, and then Arkady Tomas Cruz stepped into the dying light.

"This bloody tunnel goes on forever," muttered Billy Pilgrim, hacking away at the undergrowth crowding the narrow passageway that led deep into the observatory-temple. It had taken Finn less than ten minutes to find the site of the entranceway, but so far it had taken them almost an hour to cut their way through the tunnel, one holding the flashlight while the other chopped with the machete and the other tools Garza had left behind for them.

"Don't be such a sourpuss," answered Finn, holding the light. "This is important. This site has never been broken into. It's pristine. There's no telling what we'll find."

"Bugs," answered Billy. "There'll be bugs, and if it's not bugs it'll be snakes. Maybe both."

"Look," whispered Finn. She shone the big flashlight onto the walls. Long ago, perhaps four or five hundred years before, there had been a thick layer of mortar laid down over the heavy stones. The mortar, while still wet, had been used as the ground for a series of murals that ran along the walls at eye level. "It's the same as the Codex we found aboard the ship," said Finn. There were a number of glyphs that were clearly of Spanish soldiers and one of a man in a steel helmet but wearing a Mayan feather cloak. "Cortéz himself," murmured Finn. "It has to be."

"Can you read any more of it?"

"Not really, except that this was some sort of place used by royalty even before Cortéz arrived. That's what the glyph of the guy in the big headdress represents."

"A royal observatory?"

"Could be"—Finn nodded—"but this painting is from much later than that."

"Remind me again why we're doing this in the middle of the night in the middle of a revolution in the middle of the jungle?" Billy asked, stopping for a rest, hands on his knees, panting from the effort of cutting through the roots and undergrowth within the tunnel.

"Garza needs a place for the plutonium cores," answered Finn. "Which means we need to find a cenote under this temple."

"Oh, right." Bill nodded weakly. "The plutonium cores from the hydrogen bombs that appear to be in the hands of a Mexican drug lord." He lifted the machete and started hacking at the undergrowth again. "How do you get involved in these things, Fiona? Explain it to me again." The young British lord heaved a heartfelt sigh. "Last time it was secret codes in Rembrandts and typhoons, the time before that it was scorpions in the Libyan desert and sunken cruise ships, and before that I'm given to understand it was stolen Michelangelos under the streets of New York." He shook his head. "Takes real skill, that sort of thing."

"Just lucky, I guess," she answered. "Keep digging."

"Bollocks," grunted Billy. He took a swipe with the blade and the floor suddenly dropped out from underneath his feet and he promptly disappeared.

"We are here for the bombs down there," said Garza flatly, speaking in English.

"Mexican, yes?" Arkady said.

"Centro de Investigación y Seguridad Nacional."

"Ah." Arkady kept the dark gray Makarov pistol steady on Garza's midsection.

And you—" Garza asked. "*Cubano, sí?*"

"*Sí, da.*"

"One of those." Garza nodded.

"One of those," said Arkady. "A brown Russian. Sometimes called a Rubano."

"And the Chinese?"

"Friends of mine."

"Here for the bombs."

"That's what Guzman thinks."

"Guzman. Angel Guzman? The drug lord."

"That's not what he calls himself."

"You said thinks."

"He's out of his mind. Maniacs shouldn't have hydrogen bombs. Stalin and the hydrogen bomb couldn't coexist on the same planet. Stalin had to go."

"You sound sure of yourself."

"I'm half Russian. We know these things, us Russians."

"Why should I believe you?" Garza said.

"In the first place, I'm the one with the gun. In the second place, why would I lie when I could just shoot you instead." Arkady looked at the other two. "Who are they?"

"Friends. Part of an archaeological expedition that got in the way of some rather large ants."

"We heard they were nearby. Guzman thinks they're monsters created by his bombs. He says it's a sign he's meant to be king of Mexico."

"Idi Amin of the Yucatán."

"Something like that."

"So now what do we do?"

"You could put down the gun for a start."

Arkady lowered his weapon slightly.

"So, now what?"

"We work together. There's a temple, an observatory about a mile or so away from here. Where the bombs were."

"I know it."

"These people have some friends who're sure the temple is built on top of a hidden cenote. You bring along the cores of the bombs and we sink them there."

"We were going to blow up the cores right here, get rid of the bombs and Guzman at the same time."

"And turn a few square miles of my country into an irradiated wasteland?"

Arkady shrugged. "Not a Cuban wasteland, however. Not my problem."

"No. Mine."

"You have a way to detonate the casings?"

"In the backpack."

"We were going to booby-trap the high-explosive triggers."

"And get away in time?"

"It would be close. My Chinese friends are fairly sure, however."

"It would cause a great deal of trouble if your Oriental friends were captured. International trouble."

"Or a Cuban." Arkady smiled. "Especially one who is half Russian."

"Best to avoid it if possible, especially since our goals are the same. Or so you say."

"You doubt me?" Arkady asked.

"I doubt everything," said Garza. "That's the business I'm in." The Mexican paused. "A truce?"

"For the time being," said Arkady. "Until we figure this thing out. A truce."

25

"Billy!"

For a few moments there was nothing and then Finn heard a faint groan.

"Billy! Are you all right?!"

"Of course I'm all right. I just fell through the floor of a Mayan temple and cracked my head on a great bloody slab of polished rock. God knows, perhaps it's the bloody carapace of a giant bloody mutated bug that's about to swallow me whole, but I wouldn't bloody well know, would I, because it's dark as granny's foot locker down this bloody rabbit hole, isn't it?"

He groaned again.

Finn laughed out loud. If he could grumble like that he wasn't badly hurt. She took a length of rope out of the pack Garza had left and tied it firmly to a thick twist of root protruding through the wall of the corridor.

"I'm coming down," she warned. She tossed the end of the rope down through the ragged hole in the floor of the passageway. She threw the pack over one shoulder, clipped the end of the flashlight tether to her belt, turned, and began to lower herself through the hole.

The bottom was covered in a heavy layer of vegetative undergrowth that had intruded over the centuries, as well as the crumbled, thin limestone blocks that Billy had fallen through, weakened by dampness and the passage of time. Finn unclipped the flashlight and shone it around the chamber. The room was large, at least fifteen or twenty feet long and half as wide, the ancient ceiling twelve feet above them. The wall she faced was bare except for a single glyph in the center in a perfect circle. At first glance it appeared to show some sort of spiraling design. She turned the light away, searching for Billy.

The light found him sitting slumped on a shelf in the rock wall, rubbing his knee. Behind him on the near wall was the huge painted figure of a jaguar.

"Well, here we are then," said Billy. "The question is, where is here?"

"A burial chamber," said Finn without hesitation. Her heart began to pound with excitement. "I think you're sitting on the occupant."

Billy jumped up as though the stone beneath him was red-hot. Finn shone the light down.

"Dear God," she whispered.

The shelf Billy had been using as a seat was actually the top of a huge rectangular stone box. The box, a sarcophagus, was made out of huge sheets of quarried limestone.

It stood at least four feet high and virtually filled one end of the chamber, making it ten or twelve feet long. The side panels and the lid were intricately painted and carved, the colors as fresh and bright as they'd been laid down in the wet mortar half a millennium before.

The designs were classic, bats, jaguars, and birds swirling in wonderful patterns, a Mayan king in the center wearing a huge feathered headdress of office and carrying a ceremonial shield and spear. His chest was covered in a breastplate of jade squares and he wore a jade helmet in the shape of a snarling jaguar's head. On his belt was an ornate obsidian sword, and in his other hand an obsidian fighting club.

One arm was raised, pointing at the far end of the massive lid, where something that looked vaguely like an old-fashioned Mercury space capsule arced through the sky trailing fire.

"Eric somebody or other," said Billy as Finn's light lingered.

"Von Daniken," Finn answered. "*Chariots of the Gods.* He had a weird theory about ancient spaceships. Historical UFOs. It's actually a Mayan representation of the planet Venus, which they thought was a star. Almost all Mayan and Aztec cosmology is based on the transit of Venus across the equator. It made for almost perfect mathematical accuracy."

"Don't ask me," said Lord Billy. "I needed a tutor to get me a bare pass on my R-level maths." The Englishman paused. "Although it seems to me that he's pointing to that round thingee on the wall."

Finn shone the flashlight on the large round glyph she'd spotted when she first lowered herself into the burial chamber.

It was at least two feet in diameter, and even on close examination looked like the whorled imaginative doodling of a bored schoolchild. To the left were a series of ladderlike spirals that went down to a narrow rectangle, and from a circular pattern in the center of the rectangle a whole series of interlocking angled patterns twisted and turned in a complex maze that led to another circle in the upper right. Both of the circular areas were marked by the flat outlined shape of a hand. Finn had seen a lot of Mayan hieroglyphs but never one like this.

"Can you read it?" Billy asked.

"Not even close," said Finn, shaking her head.

"Maybe it's not supposed to mean anything at all," offered Billy.

"Unlikely," said Finn. "This is a royal tomb. Anything here is here for a reason."

"No cenote pool."

"Gee, I hadn't noticed," said Finn, continuing to examine the circular pattern.

"I thought it was only cavemen who used hand patterns like that," said Billy.

"It's common to most cultures, certainly Mesoamericans."

"I used to draw things like that in school," mused Billy. "Especially in classes I didn't much care for. Calculus and demotic Greek. Mr. Pieman."

"Pieman?"

"We used to call him Simple. You know, Simple Simon met a pieman going to the fair…"

"I got it the first time round." Finn laughed.

"Everyone used to draw those. We'd hand them around and see who could work out the most complicated mazes."

"That's it," said Finn, staring at the ancient circular drawing painted on the wall.

"That's what?" Billy asked.

"It's a maze. A map. That snaky thing is almost certainly the staircase in the observatory tower up above us. The rectangle is the burial vault. That other circle at the end of the maze pattern could be the cenote."

"But where do we start?" Billy asked. "How do we get into the maze? I can't see any way out of here."

Finn stepped forward and stared at the map on the wall. The hand outline on the glyph was located in the center of the circular pattern laid over the rectangle. The hand on the hieroglyphic was the hand she was looking at right now. Tentatively she reached up and placed her own hand over the outline drawn five hundred years before. It was an eerily accurate fit.

"Press here," she murmured. And she did. There was a deep-throated groaning noise, as though the very earth around them was in pain, and then the huge circular glyph rotated on hidden hinges, revealing the dark entrance to a tunnel behind the wall.

"Cheeky buggers," said Billy, staring at the yawning hole. "Hiding that there all this time."

Finn could feel a faint cool breeze against her cheek.

"This leads to the outside."

"We're not going in there, are we?" Billy said. "What about the others? How will they manage to find us?"

"Didn't I see some glow sticks in the pack Garza left us?"

"What about it?"

"We leave a trail of bread crumbs for them to follow. If we're going to find deep water for those plutonium cores, it's the only way."

Billy dug around in the pack and came out with a handful of the eight-inch-long batons. He counted them.

"Eighteen."

"That should do. Crack one and let's get moving."

Billy sighed. He bent one of the plastic sticks, breaking the fragile interior glass vial inside and activating the chemical reaction. A soft green glow filled the cavernous chamber. Finn gripped the flashlight and stepped through the hole. Heaving the pack onto his back, Billy followed, sighing.

"Half a league, half a league, half a league onward, all in the valley of Death rode the six hundred. 'Forward, the Light Brigade! Charge for the guns!' he said: Into the valley of Death rode the six hundred."

"Oh, shut up," said Finn.

26

"This is definitely not going to work," muttered Eli Santoro, pulling the fatigue cap lower over his eyes as he marched with the others across the compound.

"I thought all you Americans were positive thinkers," said Arkady Cruz, leading Eli and Guido across to the far palisade and one of the shacklike huts against the gate-side wall. Cruz had found the two outsiders the proper uniforms for members of Angel Guzman's little army and was now preparing to arm them to the teeth.

"Eyes left," said Cruz under his breath. Eli looked. Beside the shack were a line of three of the roughly armored jungle buggies the soldiers used to get around in.

"Can you drive that?" Cruz asked.

"Yes."

"What about you?" Cruz asked Guido, who towered over Cruz and was larger than any one of Guzman's soldiers Cruz had seen so far.

"*Positief.*" The big Dutchman nodded. "*Makkelijk.*"

"Let's hope that means yes," said the submarine captain.

"It does," said Garza. "What's the plan?"

"We get you into the weapons hut, pick up a few things we're going to need, then make like John Wayne in *Fort Apache*."

"What?" Eli said, startled.

"*Fort Apache, She Wore a Yellow Ribbon, Rio Grande*. You know, Howard Hawks's cavalry trilogy. What kind of an American are you, gringo?"

"What kind of a Cuban are you?" Eli responded.

"One who watches a lot of old movies on boring patrols." Cruz laughed. He jogged up three rickety steps and ducked through the open doorway of the makeshift armory. The tin-roofed shed smelled of hot metal and gun oil. It was also very dark.

Eli could just make out racks of weapons and shelves loaded with wooden and cardboard boxes of ammunition. Cruz handed Eli and Guido identical weapons. They looked like old-fashioned wood-stock AK-47s with a flare gun strapped on underneath, giving the forward area under the barrel its own trigger. The description wasn't far off.

"Russian GP-30 grenade launchers," said Cruz, handing them over along with the canvas sacks full of projectiles. "Jam a round down the barrel until you hear a click, then squeeze the trigger. Make sure you put the stock against your shoulder before you fire or you'll blow your arm off. Effective range is about a hundred and fifty yards. Got it?"

"Got it." Eli nodded.

"Got it," said Guido, who had used something much like it when he had been among the last Dutchmen to be inducted into the army for two years of national service back in the late '90s.

He took one of the stumpy-looking 40mm grenades, slid it into the barrel, and turned it expertly in the socket. It clicked loudly.

"Good," said Cruz. He handed Garza a bazooka-like RPG rocket for himself. "I'll drive the first buggy with you as my passenger," he said, nodding to Garza. "You take out the big half-round hut with the RPG as a distraction and we pick up one of my Chinese friends with the cores.

"You, American, come in behind me and pick up the man with the second core. Dutchman, you come third and pick up the last two men. One of them is the leader. His name is Wong Fei Hung, but he answers to Colonel.

"Guy with a nasty scar on his face. He's already armed, except Guzman doesn't know it. He and his companion will have set the charges you brought with you. The colonel's job is to take out Guzman if he gets the opportunity. We go out through the main gate firing and hope your friends have found a way to get rid of the cores and save us from Guzman's wrath. He cut a guy in half yesterday with a machete. Not pleasant."

"Great pep talk," muttered Eli.

"Go, Yankees." Cruz grinned. He headed out of the shack and back into the compound, the three men behind him. None of the other soldiers in the fort seemed to be paying any attention. There was no sign of Guzman. The four Chinese were still clustered around the fly tent in front of the Quonset hut.

"Any signal to let this colonel know we're ready?" Eli asked, glancing nervously around the compound. Too many men, too many guns.

"The first shot," said the Cuban. "Now, let's vamos!"

Without the slightest hesitation Cruz clambered into the nearest jungle buggy, motioned Garza into the canvas-strapped seat beside him, and fired up the ignition. Garza tried to make the RPG as unobtrusive as possible, but it was hard to be discreet with a rocket launcher. No one paid the slightest attention. Eli climbed into the second buggy and fired up the roaring, unmuffled engine. Maybe they did this every night, a dusk patrol of the perimeter.

Behind him Eli heard Guido start up the third buggy. There was a roar as the John Wayne Cuban let out a bloodcurdling wail and sped off in a cloud of dust, and after that things started moving unbelievably quickly.

Just keeping the bouncing, leaping, slewing jungle buggy behind Cruz was hard enough, but he was vaguely aware of the bulky shape of Garza half standing in his canvas seat in the forward buggy, aiming the RPG toward the Quonset hut.

There was a huge hand-clapping explosion, a six-foot tongue of flame from the rear of the RPG, and almost magically the Quonset hut seemed to lift completely off the ground and disintegrate in front of his eyes. Eli was vaguely aware of seeing one of the Chinese technicians grab something off the trestle table and dive into the rear of the buggy, and then it was his turn.

He dragged his buggy around just in time for the second technician to vault into the seat beside him. Without a word the man picked up the grenade launcher, loaded it and hunkered down in his seat, balancing the fat flare gun barrel on the edge of the door frame.

He was barely aware of the sound of rapid firing and then, as they swung toward the main gate, he saw a short potbellied figure appear on the front porch of the big tin-roofed headquarters building.

The man had a pistol in his hand and a look of uncomprehending fury on his round, Charlie Brown face, centered with a silly mustache fifty years out of style. Then, almost magically, with cartoonish idiocy, the face sucked in on itself and then disappeared in an amazing explosion of flowering brains, blood, and other associated tissue that looked as though the drug lord's neck had suddenly turned into an active volcano.

The headless corpse stood for a moment, then crumpled like a puppet with its strings cut. Beside him Eli's passenger steadied the grenade launcher, aimed it over the heads of Cruz and Garza, then fired. There was a hard cracking noise and Eli actually saw the grenade loop over the lead buggy's front end and crash into the front gate.

There was a scream from somewhere and out of the corner of his eye again Eli saw his passenger actually pulled out of his seat and thrown to the ground by the force of the round that had killed in a split second. There was no time to mourn or even be afraid. Directly ahead of him the palisade gate turned into a sheet of flame as the grenade exploded, and then he was out of the compound, heading down the narrow track into the jungle, swallowed by the night. The fight was over. The chase was on.

27

Finn shone the beam of the flashlight into the opening. The floor of the passage was split and wet, evidence that water flowed down it regularly. There seemed to be another passage as well, part of the maze, a low oval tunnel, which, if they chose it, would force them to walk stooped over.

"Time to play *Jeopardy*! again?" Billy asked, coming up beside her. Since joining the crew of the *Hispaniola* he'd become a devoted fan of Alex Trebek and the addictive show. "I'm for the main fissure."

"That's because you don't want to bend over," said Finn.

"No," said Billy. "That's because the main fissure is wet, and I thought water was what we were looking for."

"Point."

"Thank you."

Finn shone the flashlight into the narrower slot and then followed the beam, Billy close behind, dropping a second glow stick just inside the entrance to mark their way. Almost instantly Billy regretted his choice; the clammy walls of the fissure were only inches from his shoulders. If he deviated at all from the exact center of the tunnel his arms brushed the walls, each touch claustrophobically reminding him of what a cramped space he was in. He tried to keep his eyes fixed on the bobbing of Finn's light ahead of him, gritting his teeth against the screams of panic he'd like to release. Cramped spaces were definitely not his forte.

As they progressed, small streams of water joined the tiny trickle on the floor, seemingly coming out of nowhere, oozing out of almost invisible cracks in the limestone in the walls and ceiling of the passage. Twenty minutes in they were up to their knees. Billy crammed another glow stick into a wider crack in the wall.

"What do we do if it gets any deeper?"

"Swim," answered Finn, grinning back at him, but he knew she was worried too. They slogged on. Billy could feel the tension and his claustrophobia increasing.

"Try reciting the multiplication tables. It takes your mind off things," said Finn.

"I told you maths was never my subject."

"Decline a few Latin verbs then."

"*Amo, amas, amat, amamus, amatus, amant.*"

"What's that?"

"To love."

"Try something else."

"*Ad praesens ova cras pullis sunt meliora.*"

"What in the name of heaven is that?"

"Eggs today are better than chickens tomorrow."

"A bird in the hand is worth two in the bush?"

"Something like that."

"Quiet!"

"*Silentium*."

"No, really."

"*Profecto*."

"Shut up and listen!"

Billy finally got the message. He stopped in his tracks and listened.

"What?"

"An echo," said Finn, excitement rising in her voice.

"What does that mean?"

"The fissure widens somewhere ahead. A cave. The cenote. Maybe where all this water drains."

"Then let's get going," said Billy. They moved forward. Within a few feet the fissure began to narrow even more, the cold water pushing hard against the backs of their legs. Billy was forced to reach out and grab the slimy limestone walls for whatever grip he could find to keep from being bowled over by the rushing stream. As they went farther down, even the walls seemed to come together. At first Billy thought it was his fevered imagination conjuring up more Indiana Jones-style fantasies, but then he realized that the nightmare was real. The walls really were closing in on him. Within a few minutes they could no longer walk face-on and had to shuffle sideways, their noses to the wall only a few inches away. As the passage narrowed, the water naturally rose until it was frothing under their armpits. Billy knew he couldn't take much more. His teeth began to chatter.

"You okay?" Finn asked, turning back to him, the light shining brightly.

"Just keep going," he grated, pushing onward.

A second later the light disappeared and Billy gasped with horror, terrified that Finn had vanished into some unseen pothole in front of them. Then the light reappeared and the sound of the water seemed to increase by a thousand percent. Billy took a stumbling step forward and suddenly he was out of the fissure and standing in a huge open cave, the water rushing out of the crack behind them as though it was spilling from a broken pipe. Finn swung the light around.

"Where are we?"

"Heaven, I think," said Finn, her voice filled with awe.

The cavern was no bigger than a large single-family house, rising three stories up to a roof that had vanished long ago. Directly overhead was only the dark night sky, the stars like a wash of fire, the entire drift of the Milky Way laid out before them. At their feet, perhaps ten feet below the ledge they stood on, was the pool of the cenote, the rush of water from their fissure gushing out in a miniature waterfall. Directly in front of them, rising out of the water like one of the mysterious jet-black slabs in the film *2001*, was a massive plate of natural obsidian, the black volcanic glass that abounded in the Yucatán and that the Mayans and the Aztecs had valued so highly for its frightening ability to keep a sharp, weapon-grade edge. The obsidian slab was at least twenty feet across and almost perfectly circular, an extrusion of the broad limestone pedestal it sat upon in the center of the cenote. Even from where she stood Finn could see the delicate etching on the highly polished reflective face of the volcanic glass, reflecting each and every star in the night sky above.

"A scrying mirror," said Finn, staring.

"Scrying?" Billy asked.

"Divination. Look in the glass and see the future, which is presumably exactly what our dead king back there did. Most cultures have some form of it. Even the Mormons have a version. With a huge mirror like that you could track the stars, navigate, predict astronomical events. You could turn yourself into a god as far as the average Mayan in the street was concerned."

Finn shone the light on the wall behind them. There was a large, roughly constructed limestone seat, or throne, and behind it a neatly carved design in the limestone wall. It was a graphic representation of a star field like the one reflected in the gigantic, naturally occurring obsidian bowl.

"He'd sit in the throne and watch the stars," mused Finn. "Just like a modern-day astronomer." It was a fascinating image, two astronomers across a millennia, staring into the night sky.

"Well, your astronomer king didn't make that," said Billy, pointing at the star-field design. "Look."

Finn turned the flashlight on the stone image. There was an inscription at its base:

FRANCISCO DE ULLOA FECIT

"Francisco de Ulloa made this," translated Billy. "So it's not the guy in the coffin back there."

"No," said Finn, a faint smile growing. "It's not."

She shone the light across the etched image of the star field. It was close to that of the one etched on the obsidian mirror but somehow different. Her smile broadened.

"A treasure map," she said softly. "A really for truly treasure map."

"Of what?" Billy said.

"The way to find the lost treasure of Hernán Cortéz, the millions in gold and jewels he was holding back from the Spanish Inquisition."

Billy jumped as something hit the ground a few feet away from where he was standing.

"What the hell?" The bottom of a rope ladder dangled in front of them.

A moment later Eli Santoro, grinning from ear to ear, appeared in front of their startled eyes.

"How did you find us?" Finn asked.

"Apparently our Mexican friend didn't quite trust us. He had a GPS beacon hidden in the pack he left you. All we did was follow it."

"Sneaky bugger!" Billy grunted.

"What about this Guzman guy?" Finn asked. "The bombs?"

"A Chinese guy blew his brains out. Amazing shot. Without anyone to lead them the rest of them headed for the hills," said Eli blandly. "You have any interesting little adventures while we were gone?"

"One or two," said Finn with equal bland-ness. "One or two."

28

"Okay, you'd better run this by us again," said Billy. "Because it's still a little difficult for us to see the connection between a five-hundred-year-old observatory in the jungles of the Yucatán and bobbing around in the polluted waters of a man-made lake in the middle of the California desert that didn't exist before 1906." The British lord glanced around; they were completely landlocked. To the west were the Santa Rosa Mountains. The Chocolate Mountains were to the east and the Coachella Valley to the north. They were about a hundred miles inland from Baja California's Sea of Cortéz.

The treasure seekers were sitting under a canvas awning on the rear deck of the ancient houseboat they'd rented from the Bombay Shores Marina at the southern end of the lake. "Marina" was quite a stretch since they had only a ten-foot dock and one other boat for rent. Then again, "houseboat" was a stretch, too. It looked more like a 1950s two-toned aluminum-sided trailer home on a leaky barge, which was probably a pretty accurate description of the craft that the owner had named the *Clarabelle*.

There were four of them on board: Finn, Billy, Guido, and Briney Hanson to operate the dredging equipment for them. Eli Santoro, wearing scuba gear and manhandling the vacuum dredge into position, had the unsavory task of being the chosen diver for the day. The water in the lake was a deep and chemical brown, the surface dotted here and there with belly-up dead fish.

Arkady Cruz, sensing a certain lack of appreciation for his new alliances in Mexico, had prudently decided to defect and was now a full-fledged member of the *Hispaniola*'s crew in Nassau. He was now teaching Run-Run McSeveney, the half-Chinese, half-Scot engineer, how to swear in colloquial Cuban.

"Perhaps you could start with this Spaniard," suggested Guido.

"Francisco de Ulloa," said Finn.

"The very fellow," said Billy.

"The one who drew the map, yes?" Guido asked.

"That's him," said Finn. She unrolled a small-scale chart of the Sea of Cortéz and Baja on the rickety card table between them. "He was a friend of Cortéz. Early on he acted as a courier for him between Cuba and Spain, carrying letters to Cortéz's wife.

"Anyway, Cortéz realized that King Charles and the Inquisition were plotting to steal his treasure and have him excommunicated, so he commissioned Ulloa to take the gold and jewelry from the hoard he'd seized from

Montezuma, the Aztec king he'd conquered in what is now Mexico City, and find a place to hide it well away from prying eyes.

"Nobody is entirely sure, but what is known is that the Spaniard sailed from Acapulco in three small ships built especially for the expedition. They headed north into what we now call the Sea of Cortéz, which Ulloa named in honor of his patron.

"They reached the head of the Baja Peninsula and found what some people think was the original outlet for the Colorado River. He left two of his ships in the mouth of the river, then took the largest ship, the one carrying the treasure itself, and headed upriver looking for a good hiding place.

"Before he could find a good spot there was a serious earthquake—the San Andreas Fault is only a few miles from here—and there was a tidal wave almost forty feet high that rushed in from the Sea of Cortéz.

"The two ships at the mouth of the river rode the wave out easily enough, but the treasure ship was taken inland on the surge. Almost a hundred miles. When the water receded the ship was left high and dry in the middle of a desert—what was then known as the Salton Sink, a salt basin like Salt Lake City but even lower than Death Valley.

"The ship was half buried in the sand. Ulloa finished the job with his men and then walked back to the other two ships. That's how the Legend of the Lost Ship of the

Desert was born. There were a bunch of sightings over the years as the sands shifted. In 1906 a section of the Imperial Irrigation Canal on the Colorado River collapsed and the river flooded into the old Salton Sink for two years. It put almost four hundred square miles underwater before they could stop the flow. It's been underwater and getting more and more polluted ever since."

"I still don't see the connection to the map you found," said Briney Hanson, lighting one of his spiced clove cigarettes.

"I think Ulloa took one of the Mayan astronomers with him," she said. "It's the only theory that fits. There are more than a hundred stars a pilot can use to navigate by; the Mayans knew almost fifty of them, as well as the moon transit, the transit of the sun, and the transit of Venus across the night sky. Given enough reference points, which the map on the wall shows, coming up with the location wasn't that difficult."

"So you matched the plot of the map on the wall of the cave with a computer simulation?" Briney asked.

"That's right." Finn nodded. "A simulation of the night sky in the Yucatán, the night sky variance with the Sea of Cortéz in 1539, the year Ulloa made his voyage, and a star plot of the same sky now. Thirty-three degrees North by one hundred and fifteen degrees west. Simple."

"Easy for you," muttered Billy.

"Which is right here?" Guido said.

"Give or take a hundred yards or so," said Briney. "The portable side-scanning radar shows a heavy metal mass directly below us. The water's only eighteen feet deep."

"You really think it's the treasure ship?" Billy asked skeptically "You said there were entire towns flooded back in 1906."

"It's worth a look." Finn shrugged.

"Let us not make it too long a look," said Guido, wrinkling his nose. "I have never smelled anything so bad."

The Dutchman was right. The temperature on the lake was well over one hundred degrees and the smell of dead fish and pollution was foul. Almost on cue there was a tug on the signal line that connected down to Eli's position underwater. Briney Hanson stood up and went to the big compressor they'd bolted to the rear deck and switched it on. There was a grumbling, almost visceral intestinal sound and the heavy plastic vacuum tube began to swell in its wire braces as the pumps began to work, drawing up sand and silt from the bottom. The snout of the tube was fitted over a wire cage that would catch anything sucked up from underwater.

Eli Santoro's wet-suited figure came to the surface. He pulled off his mask, tossed it onto the deck, and climbed up the short ladder. He stood on the deck, a look of utter revulsion on his face. His wet suit was covered in gray-brown slime. He smelled like an open sewer.

"It's absolutely disgusting down there," he grunted, breathing hard.

"Find anything?" Finn asked.

"About six feet of muck, a layer of dead, rotting fish." He paused and reached into the small net pouch on his belt. "And this." He grinned. He tossed the object down onto the center of the old card table. The vacuum pump made a gurgling sound as though something was stuck in its throat. The object from Eli's pouch gleamed dully on the table. It was roughly oval, a quarter of an inch thick, and about as big as a small dinner plate. In the center was a roughly stamped Spanish cross and an equally rough date stamp: 1521. The plate was solid gold. A thousand years before the date stamped on it, the gold had been a sculpted image of Kukulcan, the winged god of creation the Maya had worshipped while the Spanish people were Iberian hunter-gatherers lurking in caves.

"The treasure of Cortéz."

At seven p.m. Atlantic time the following evening, a Cessna Mustang business jet registered to Noble Pharmaceutical disappeared over the Gulf of Mexico. According to the manifest the only passenger was James Jonas Noble, head of the giant pharmaceutical corporation and father of Harrison Noble, the play-boy adventurer who had recently disappeared while leading an archaeological expedition in the Yucatán. Foul play was not ruled out in the disappearance of the drug tycoon's jet. There was some thought that it might have accidentally wandered into Cuban airspace and been shot down. Cuban authorities refused to comment.

Two hours after the disappearance of James Jonas Noble, Cardinal Enrico Rossi of the Vatican secretary of state's office and one of the senior directors of the Banco Venizia, an arm of the Vatican Bank in Rome, died at his desk, apparently of a massive heart attack. He was seventy-seven years old and was known to have smoked two packages of Marlboro cigarettes per day. The Pope, an old friend of Rossi's, had ordered a high requiem mass to be said for Rossi three days later. In an allied story, Claudio Succi, an investigative reporter for the Italian newspaper *Il Tempo Roma*, was the victim of a hit and run in the early hours of the evening. Succi was known to have been working on a story about corruption at the Vatican Bank with Cardinal Rossi as its central focus. Succi's laptop computer was demolished as a result of the accident. No trace of the driver or the vehicle was found.

Two days after the death of Cardinal Rossi and the unfortunate journalist, Claudio Succi, Francis Xavier Sears, the professional serial killer for hire, met with Max Kessler, the information provider and blackmailer, on one of the benches close to the Smithsonian. It was another gorgeous day in Washington, D.C., although a little too humid for Max Kessler's taste. While he waited for Sears he nibbled a chocolate biscotti and sipped his Ethiopian blend coffee from the Farragut Square Starbucks. Sears, wearing a plain dark suit and cheap shoes, appeared at exactly noon; right on time, as usual. He was carrying a copy of the *Washington Times* folded in one hand, their agreed-upon signal that the coast was clear. Kessler smiled as Sears sat down on the bench beside him. He appreciated punctuality almost above all other things.

"Things went well, I assume."

"That they did." Sears nodded.

"No trouble with the cardinal?"

"No."

"Or the journalist? Bit of a snag there."

"No."

"Nice touch with Noble's plane, the Cuban involvement."

"Yes."

"Biscotti?" Kessler inquired, offering Sears a brown paper bag. He'd purchased two of the crunchy morsels to celebrate.

"No, thanks," murmured Sears.

"I read about Ms. Ryan's find in the Salton Sink in the *Post* today. Quite a coup."

"Yes."

"No sign of the Celatropamine sample?"

"No."

"How soon before the news about the drug leaks?"

"Less than a month."

"Plenty of time to sell the stock short."

"Yes."

"This will make us both extremely wealthy. A coup for us as well as Ms. Ryan and her friends." Kessler smiled. "All the loose ends dealt with."

"Almost," said Sears.

"Almost?"

"One more," murmured Sears. Without haste, he unfolded the newspaper in his lap, brought out the six-inch undertaker's trocar hypodermic and jammed it unerringly into Kessler's left ear hole. The needle went in fully and Sears pushed the plunger fully inward before withdrawing the slim needle. Kessler died instantly, his eyes bugging out ever so briefly. The barrel of the syringe had been loaded with fresh blood Sears had drawn from his own veins less than an hour before. He laid the empty syringe down in his lap and folded the newspaper over it again. The entire operation, performed in public, had taken seventeen seconds. No one had paid the slightest attention.

A cursory autopsy would show that Kessler had died of a cerebral hemorrhage, a stroke not being an untoward death for a man who had consumed as much artery-clogging cholesterol as the nasty little German. A more careful forensically inclined examination would show the path of the trocar needle into Kessler's ear, but who cared? Kessler had enough enemies to keep an FBI task force in business for the next century. Just his legendary file cards would keep them busy for decades.

Sears thought about the file cards for a moment, wondering if Kessler had kept one on him. Almost certainly. He stared at the man's cooling corpse beside him, then reached into Kessler's pocket and found a set of keys. He'd do the world and himself a favor. Arson wasn't a specialty of his, but he could put together a decent fire in a pinch.

"One last loose end," he said. He pocketed the keys and stood up. He paused, then reached into the bag on the bench beside the dead man. "Maybe I'll have that biscotti after all," he said, then turned and walked away.

The Finn Ryan Conspiracy Thrillers

Michelangelo's Notebook

The Lucifer Gospel

Rembrandt's Ghost

The Aztec Heresy